C000174619

Grey and Scarlet 1: The Grey Lady Ghost of the Cambridge Military

Hospital.

By

C.G Buswell

Copyright © 2015 C.G.Buswell

Also by C.G. Buswell

Novels

Grey and Scarlet 2: The Drummer Boy (Out November

2016)

Short Stories

Christmas at Erskine

Halloween Treat

For Karla, a fellow QA who has blessed me with friendship, love, marriage and much joy.

1

She sat alone, waiting patiently, in the dark, but for the light of the half-moon filtering through the tall windows. Her long bony fingers smoothed the invisible creases of her dark grey nursing uniform and white apron. The walls danced to the movement from the light wind on the overgrown bushes outside and those that sought refuge through the neglected cracks in the walls that brushed against the peeling paint that flaked in clumps to the floor. Foxes barked their harrowing calls of the night as they sought the comfort of another whilst the rats scratched along the wooden floors in search of food, little knowing that they would be easy prey for the owl that in turn looked over her, aware of her presence, but not seeing her, only sensing. Soon there would be new souls to care for, to help ease their passage and bring some comfort from the pain of life. These past few years she never understood where her patients had gone, but soon her ward would once again have a new patient for her to tend, she sensed this and waited.

'Dicker on the roof!' barked Sergeant Buchan into his personal role radio to the other members of his eight strong section of 4 Scots. Instinctively all of his men of The Royal Regiment of Scotland checked that their safety catches of their SA80 A2 rifles remained off as they neared the compound, wishing they were back in the safety of their Mastiff along with the two crew left to protect the vehicle as they searched the area. Even Corporal Naomi Scarlet, their medic, from the Royal Army Medical Corps, on secondment from 2 Medical Regiment, automatically did her checks knowing that contact could be imminent. Only for her it was the ritualistic checking of tourniquets, clamps, heavy duty field scissors and med packs strapped to the front of her chest rig. This check, check and check again ritual was drilled into her by Staff Sergeant Taffy Williams during her combat medical technician trade training at Keogh Barracks in Ash Vale near Aldershot. He was a veteran of the First Gulf War and his instruction and experience had proved useful

6

for Cpl Scarlet saving several squaddies lives in the second Gulf War back in 2006. Though with the horrific injuries they sustained she was never sure if she was doing them a favour, they were nicknamed the unexpected survivors. Now, due to advanced trauma support, around 80% of battlefield casualties survived. This automatic medical equipment check done, she then looked through the sight unit small arms trilux of her SA80 to see what the drama was.

'The wee fucker,' swore Private Clarke into the PPR with great anger that only the broad brogue of a Peterhead lad can vocalise in few words, 'the wee rag head looks only twelve.'

'Aye, about the same mental age as you Andy!' joked Private Fraser McAllister, the youngest and cheekiest member of the group. He was fresh out of recruit training and posted straight to The Stan as he called it in his letters home to his mother in Stonehaven.

'Enough chit chat lads', chided Corporal Billie Anderson, 'the next numptee to say anything stupid over their PPR gets put onto shit burning duty when we get back to camp.'

Private Clarke swore under his breath recalling the last time he had the privilege of this dirty job. Anyone under discipline had the horrendous job of dousing the full tin of faeces from their improvised toilet area and adding any fuel he could lay their hands on so that it could be sanitarily destroyed. Only whatever unlucky sod did this usually got covered in crap as it went up in flames, and often it had to be lit several times. Though some didn't mind the duty because it was rumoured that whoever performed this task was awarded with an extra ten pounds tax free in their wage slip when they got back to the UK. Fine and handy for going out on the piss at Mambo's in the Bloo Toon of Peterhead, so named after the rows and rows of the coloured slate roofs in the old fisherman's town. Though his auntie always argued it was because the fishermen wore blue jerseys, or ganseys as she would refer to them, when at sea so that if they fell overboard and drowned they would be recognised as coming from that area by the colour of their jumper. He was last put onto shit burning duty for falling asleep during stag duty. He knew he got off lightly since sleeping whilst on guard duty was one of the worst offences a soldier could commit since his oppos were relying on him to keep them safe while they tried to catch up on much needed sleep and downtime.

Corporal Scarlet did a double check through her SUSAT, *Christ she thought; he's younger than my brother.* Though she couldn't resist a small smile at the language Andrew had used knowing that his wife had tried banning him from using foul language since the birth of their daughter three months ago. She thought fondly of her fiancé, Scott, safely nursing at Camp Bastion Hospital, who also didn't like her swearing and the recent rude words and phrases the Jocks had taught her.

'Stay alert lads,' commanded Sergeant Buchan, 'there is a Zarang motorbike against this wall we're approaching and no-one around. That's his *get the fuck out of here* ride and we're heading into something I don't like the look of. The wee rag head is talking into a mobile, something's about to kick off. I bet my big right ball that the fucker is letting the flip-flops know all about us.' He was starting to regret not having a squad of the Afghan National Army, useful for their local knowledge. But this was supposed to be a simple Op with no contact with civilians so no need for an interpreter, and minimum troops needed.

The eight person strong patrol inched closer to the compound, walking carefully for signs of an improvised explosive device and other booby traps, grateful for Corporal Stewart, their ordinance and explosives expert leading the way, sweeping his metal detector, searching constantly with large sweeps close to the ground, knowing that at all times his mates had his back. 'Rory and Ewan, I want you two to set up the Minimi by that low wall where Corporal Stewart is sweeping, cover us as we enter the building,' ordered Sergeant Buchan over the PPR.

'Right boss,' replied Private Morrison, nodding to Private Young as they moved with caution over the hard ground to the low mud wall, giving them a commanding view down into the compound and surrounding fields. Their intended target was inside the compound, which intelligence revealed was deserted, but had a cache of enemy weapons. Their operation today was to seek them out and guard Corporal Stewart as he blew the weapons up to deny their use to the enemy. They knelt down on the packed earth, grateful for the knee pads over their combat trousers to give some protection from the sharp stones that seemed to populate the area. They also acted as a barrier between the ever present goat faeces that seemed to be abundant in this area along with the ubiquitous flies that they attracted. Despite being caked dry by the sun the dung always seemed to be moist and stinking in the middle, especially when knelt upon.

The rest of the patrol followed carefully in the footsteps of Corporal Stewart, their SA80's at the ready as he listened intently for the change in tone which would alert him to danger. Suddenly small arms fire opened up from the main wall of the compound, a Taliban insurgent letting rip with an AK47. The troops instinctively hit the dirt and let off controlled rounds at their new target, not needing the boss to tell them where their target was, training taking over. This threat more immediate than that of IEDs. They laid down covering fire to allow Privates Morrison and Young the valuable few seconds to set up the Minimi light machine gun. Immediately there was the roaring of gunfire as their 200 rounds of belted ammunition leapt to their target, the 5.56mm rounds ripping open the wall to reveal a Taliban insurgent spraying his mates with his AK47 assault rifle. Seconds later rounds tore into his flesh, spraying the dry earth with blood, bone and small pieces of flesh as his white and blue patterned kameez turned a moist dull red. 'Aye ye Choggie gypit hoor', shouted an excited Private Young resorting to the guttural slang of his Doric mother tongue from the streets of Torry in Aberdeen combined with the nickname for the Taliban, 'take that ye bastard,' he screamed as he took his finger off the trigger and applied the safety catch 'one less raghead causing trouble in this fuck awful country.'

As Rory turned to congratulate Ewan on another enemy kill he heard a sharp ping and his face suddenly felt wet, he tasted bitter copper as he instinctively licked his suddenly wet lips in the dry heat and looked in horror as part of Ewan's eye had exploded and blood was now gushing in to fill the empty eye socket, spraying the dry foreign soil. 'Oh fuck no, man, no' he screamed as he raised his rifle in the direction of the high velocity round and shouted a warning to his mates 'Sniper. Ewan's been hit. Man down. Naomi, on me,' he screamed as he knelt down and let loose a volley of rounds to where he thought the sniper was.

All but Naomi rose as one and advanced to the enemy, firing and reloading in perfect unison, listening to Sergeant Buchan's battle commands. Instead she sprinted, despite her heavy kit, to Ewan and Rory, slinging her rifle over her shoulders and back as she ran, not feeling its weight pound upon her heavy kit with each step that seemed to take an eternity. She swiftly donned her protective clinical gloves with practiced ease as her legs carried her to her fallen comrade. Her heart sank as she saw where the sniper's round had hit Ewan, 'Oh my poor boy,' she cried as she reached him. Feeling she had to do something to show Rory that his pal had died instantly, she knelt down and felt for his carotid artery with her index and middle finger, placing them gently and reverently on his neck, close to his windpipe. She shook her head and despite the noise of battle said softly to Rory, 'I'm so sorry, he wouldn't have felt a thing.'

But as she was about to explain that his death would have been instant she heard a roar of pain and looked up to see Corporal Billie Anderson drop to the ground, his left leg spurting blood. Private Fraser McAllister shouted 'Medic, Medic!'

'Mourn later Rory: your other pals need you.' She pulled him to his feet, pointed to his rifle and despite new incoming rounds from the enemy, she raced to Billie who was writhing on the floor as Rory got himself together and joined the firefight. As she dropped down onto her knees by his thrashing body she ripped off the Velcro combat tourniquet from her chest rig. 'Alright mate, you're going to be okay.' This was the new CAT one, which she had perfected putting on within seconds during pre-deployment training, either one handed or two, back at Keogh Barracks. She never liked to think about the one handed application because that would only mean that she was applying it to herself, as all soldiers were now trained to do. No release of pressure every fifteen minutes like the old days – just immediate tightening to stem the pumping blood and let the surgeons at Camp Bastion deal with the damaged flesh, bone and nerves. 'Take the pain Billie and lie still, let me do my job mate.' She wrapped the Combat Application Tourniquet just above the wound, fresh blood furiously pumping out with the pained movement of Billie as he tried to sit up, the weight of his webbing forcing him to lie back. Naomi gagged at the sight of decimated thigh muscle and shattered bone and the smell of fresh metallic blood pumping out from his opened femoral artery as he still thrashed about in shock and pain. She ignored the spurts that splattered their warm thick liquid onto her exposed cheek and remembered her training and went through the automatic drill of MARCHP. She knew she had to control this massive haemorrhage above all else. She was used to such wounds and had seen worse injuries on her soldiers in Basra in Southern Iraq in 2006. The worst sight, that still haunted her dreams was when a militia punishment squad had cut off the fingers, ears

14

and gouged out the eyes of sympathisers of the new government. Though she was first on the scene there was nothing she could do as they had all bled out before her unit could safely approach. The support of her fiancé, Corporal Scott Grey of the Queen Alexandra's Royal Army Nursing Corps, had helped her through some dark nights. She was not going to let her friend bleed out, nor lose another comrade.

She was oblivious to all else bar her patient. She did not even realise that the sniper had now been shot dead by their own sniper, Lance Corporal Bruce Taylor, on guard at the Mastiff, but covering the backs of his mates from afar, using his bolt action L115A3 long range rifle with an impressive shot whilst the driver Pte Gary Mitchell quickly acted as spotter through his field binoculars whilst radioing through the battle and casualty update to HQ in Kandahar so that Sergeant Buchan could control the battle. Keeping as calm as possible so that no wrong information would be relayed, he gave them Corporal Anderson's and Private Young's zap numbers. These would alert Headquarters to each soldier's personal identification number with vital information for the medical teams like blood groups and allergies.

Focusing purely on the CAT, ignoring any danger she may be in, like many an RAMC medic over the years, she said to Billie who was roaring in pain and shock 'sorry mate this is going to hurt, now lie still or you'll bleed out' as she pulled the band tight and passed the tip through the buckle, where it locked in place. Billie gave a brief wince, stifled a scream and then a surprised look appeared on his face at how little pain he was now in. Naomi then twisted the rod until the metallic smelling bright red bleeding stopped. 'Now don't get too excited about this,' she tried to laugh as she felt for his distal pulse by his groin. Feeling no pulse she knew that no further bleeding out would occur. But he was still in danger of shock and infection from all the muck that would have gone into his thigh from the bullet, fragments of clothing and dirt. He needed evacuating as soon as possible but first she had to buy him the platinum ten minutes, where immediate first aid in the field by highly trained medics saved lives. Completing her first sweep of the MARCHP she automatically assessed his airway, respiratory and chest, circulation, head injury and motor function and then pain. The initial shock and surge of adrenaline from battle would now have his body pumping with natural endorphins so he wouldn't feel pain for a few minutes,

16

but when it did kick back in she knew it would be excruciating and over-whelming. So ignoring her primary health care pack she delved straight into her battlefield trauma bag for an auto-jet of morphine. In her first tour of Afghanistan she would have used a soldier's own to save her valuable supplies, never knowing when a resupply would take place. But this would have been stored in his left map pocket of his trousers so that everyone out in the field would know exactly where it was, but with so many traumatic amputations from improvised explosive devices, she no longer wasted valuable time looking, too many had been shattered along with limbs. Pulling out her scissors as she knee-crawled to his other side she cut away more of his shredded combat trousers and injected him with the 10mg of morphine deep into his muscle of his uninjured leg. 'There you go mate, that'll see you through to Camp Bastion, we'll have you safe in no time.' Pulling out her notebook and glancing at her watch she made a note of the time the tourniquet went on and the dose of morphine along with the time administered. Barely seconds had passed between both actions, so well drilled and trained was she and other CMT's.

Billie started to ramble, 'Is my dick alright? Fuck, say it is Naomi.'

He tried to sit up, but a fresh wave of nausea and pain forced him

back down onto his uncomfortable webbing. He impulsively looked

around him for his rifle, the soldier in him still trying to take part in

the battle. He gave up and resigned himself to his injury and started

to think about the future. 'Fiona won't forgive me if I don't come

home with that,' he pleaded as his right arm felt down what little

remained of his boxers and combat trousers. He was thankful that he

had been wearing his combat codpiece, the Kevlar protected

underpants issued to frontline troops three years ago. It was designed

to help protect every soldier's pelvis and groin area and was worn

outside his trousers. He hadn't realised that Naomi had already

unclipped the ultra-lightweight ballistic material during her checks

for injury and that he was worrying unnecessarily.

Naomi laughed; just as Private Knowles came sprinting over to

help, 'You Jocks, you're all the same. It's always the first question

you ask! You'll make me blush, and me an almost married girl. Yes

it is. Now keep still and tell me if you have any pain anywhere else

or feel strange at any time. You're going to be alright mate. Just

remember you owe me a beer when we meet up back in the UK.

You'll be up and walking in no time and giving Fiona the pleasure of your company. I need to radio through a sit rep so that we can get you out of here.' Only then, as she was tightly wrapping the field dressing, a celox bandage coated with chitosan, a chemical that would bind Billie's red blood cells to form a clot, over his large wound, did Naomi realise the battle had stopped. The other troops had advanced to the compound, or rather what was left of it, the motorbike buried in rubble which had a mangled arm pointed up to the sky as if trying to summon up an alternative lift home. With relief she noted its colour and civilian clothing, one less Taliban supporter. She only hoped that the mission was a success after the sacrifice of Ewan and the life changing wound Billie sustained. If the intelligence about the area being isolated and HQ only sending one small team in was wrong, was it possible that there was no arms cache, or had the Taliban returned to retrieve it? She reached for the mike of her personal role radio to talk to Private Gary Mitchell and Sergeant Buchan whose radios would reach HQ. 'Garry and Boss I need you to send a nine liner to HQ whilst I attend to Billie,' lowering her voice so as not to distress her patient, 'he's in deep trouble, you know our location etc, but please add on Cat B stretcher for Billie, Ewan didn't make it I'm afraid. He was shot clean through the eye and didn't stand a chance. There was nothing I could do. When it's safe I need two stretchers and a body bag from the Mastiff and a safe landing zone from you and the boys for the chopper.'

Category B indicated to HQ that Cpl Anderson has life threatening injuries and that he requires urgent surgical treatment. Naomi knew that he may well lose his leg, despite her best efforts and those of the Medical Emergency Response Team who would now be on their way in their specially adapted Chinook helicopter after being given the extraction go ahead by the Major in charge of the medical desk at Brigade Headquarters who would decide on priorities based on whatever else was going on in Afghanistan and what medical facility he would go to. It was up to them to get here as quickly as possible and extract Billie, to give him his golden hour, that valuable time where limb and life could be saved or lost. Though for Billie there was only one option, he needed the expertise of the surgeons at Camp Bastion, probably the finest hospital in the world and able to cope with many horrific battlefield injuries. Swift lessons had been learned over this conflict, and as with any war, medical and nursing procedures changed or were invented, many finding their usage onto

National Health Service accident and emergency units, wards and operating theatres. One such example was the use of the refrigeration unit on-board the military evacuation helicopter to safely store blood packs. It is now used by London's Air Ambulance to give civilian patients lifesaving transfusions on route to hospitals. This special fridge can store four units of O-negative blood, the blood group that can be given to anyone, and has already saved lives who would normally have bled out en-route.

The nine liner would also give vital information such as the location of the pick-up site and its security, how it would be marked and any special equipment needed. Cogs would be put into motion and because there was a fatality there would be a shut-down of communication going out until such time as Ewan's family were told the devastating news. Naomi tried not to think of poor Ewan and his parents, his father probably offshore on the rigs and his poor mum alone until her husband could be helicoptered home to Dyce Airport, no other children to comfort her.

'Will do Naomi,' came the short reply: there would be time to talk about what went on later. First they had to secure the area and bring in the extraction team. Knowing that the flight here alone would be about 14 minutes before wheels down, they grimly set about their task of making sure that the enemy were dead, their weapons made safe and the area secure. Then a flat large piece of ground would be made safe and a smoke signal lit to guide in the Royal Air Force pilot whilst two Apache attack helicopters of the Army Air Corps would hover around the area, ready to provide covering fire in the event of an attack, able to scan the ground to protect the medical personnel, troops and casualties. Besides, just like the British Army listened into the ICOM chatter of the Taliban, their leader in turn would be listening to their radio communications and they didn't want to give any valuable intel which would compromise their safety and mission away. Many a Taliban position had been identified through the Coalition listening to their Interim Communications Operations Method as a Taliban Commander talked to his men. The arms cache would have to wait – the priority was the evacuation of the wounded and the dead and the safety of the living soldiers. They would also take away the bodies of the enemy for forensic examination in the hope that they or their belongings revealed any important information.

Just after Naomi had inserted a cannula into Billie's right arm and started some vital fluid replacement, which Pte Graham Knowles was holding up, she noticed that Billie's breathing started to become laboured. 'Billie,' she shouted as she saw that he was starting to lose consciousness, 'tell me how you are feeling Billie?' She got no reply other than rasping noises through bubbles of blood in his mouth. 'Ballocks!' she exclaimed, I think he's developed a traumatic tension hemopneumothorax. Let's sit him up to see if it relieves any pressure. They took an arm each and sat him up, 'remove his webbing and lay him flat again Graham, that's not helping at all.' As they gently lowered Billie so that he was prone again Graham remembered his battlefield casualty training and knowing that Billie's kit would be going with him started to one handedly check and remove any weapons and ammunition, still carefully holding up the bag of intravenous fluid.

'You can do something about that, right?' asked a nervous Graham, the youngest of the section as he fumbled to put a clip of rounds into his own webbing.

'Yes and no,' replied an unsure Naomi as she put on a pair of stethoscopes to listen to Billie's chest. 'He's suffered a catastrophic haemorrhage and needs fresh frozen plasma from the MERT and ideally packed red blood cell transfusions, and lots of them. Blood is pooling into his lungs, causing him to have difficulty breathing. I'll do what I can, but he really needs a chest drain to relieve the pressure, re-inflate his lungs and take away what shouldn't be there.' She assured Graham and herself as she listened intently. 'Not good, but it's just his left side.'

'Have you seen this before?' asked Graham who instinctively reached out for his friend's hand and gently rubbed it whilst telling him he's going to be alright.

'Yes, but the Iraqi died from a mediastinal shift after a bad car bombing. There was nothing we could do. He died in front of us.' Seeing the look of fear suddenly appear on Graham's face she tried to sound reassuring, 'But don't worry that's not going to happen here. Billie owes me a drink! She dug into her battlefield trauma bag and took out a large needle in sterilised packing. With no time for the niceties of hand washing or disinfecting that a hospital doctor would have she ripped open Billie's combat jacket and clothing to reveal his chest. Opening the package she took out a large needle and unsheathed it. She felt along his ribs, counting to herself.

24

'Bloody hell Naomi, what are you doing with that?' demanded a shocked Graham, not knowing the meaning of half the words Naomi had said or what she was doing.

'Sorry Graham, this looks a bit brutal, but I'm about to do my first live decompression needle aspiration to his chest to relieve his intrapleural pressure. It'll make Billie breath a bit better and save his life. He's pumped up with morphine so won't feel a thing,' she said as she quickly delved into her front pouch, took out a clean latex glove and cut out the tip of the finger. She placed this over the needle. Naomi then quickly swabbed the area with a disposable surgical wipe and then stabbed the two inch needle into his chest, taking no time to add a saline filled syringe which was normal for this procedure to safely extract body fluids and air, time being of the essence, then a rush of blood and air popped out, narrowly missing Naomi's cheek. His rasping bubbly breathing soon stopped and he was breathing as normally as someone with such trauma could. She observed that the needle catheter allowed for the release of air because the latex finger from the glove fluttered as Billie exhaled. Taking her surgical tape, Naomi wrapped it around the catheter that was now sticking out from his chest wall to secure it. Pushing back her sweat soaked black fringe under her combat helmet, she then

noted down in her notepad the procedure and time and hoped that the

MERT would be here soon.

2

She walked the long corridor of the ward which seemed wider now without beds, cabinets, tables and chairs. Her silent footsteps made no indentations in the dust and there was no visible disturbance of the pieces of broken plaster from the roof. She would never grow out of the practice of moving quietly between patients during night shift and had carried that habit to this time. As she reached the double glass topped doors she imagined how her reflection would look, if her veil was straight and still white. When she pushed her way through the doors she smiled with great pride at her scarlet bands on her left sleeve, just above the white cuffs, which denoted that she was a Nursing Sister, and how proud she was to wear them. She was equally proud of her scarlet cape and often ran her fingers lovingly over her Queen Alexandra's Imperial Military Nursing Service medal and ribbon, fondly remembering receiving it from Queen Alexandra in a special ceremony alongside fellow Sisters. In her darker moments she brushed down the two service stripes that were on her right forearm, one red and one blue, each earned for one year overseas with the British Expeditionary Force in France during the Great War. She tried to avoid these memories and those of Hugh, dear sweet Hugh. Instead she continued on her journey. They were

coming and there was much preparation to be done. She glanced

down the long corridor with their shut doors to the other wards,

undisturbed for so many years, but soon to be full of people once

more, her special role in this fine military hospital fulfilled once

again. Her special gift to lost souls was once more in demand.

Scott leaned back in the chair and stretched out his arms as he arched his back to relieve the pressure from the long hours of waiting. He was beginning to feel older than his 32 years but was glad of this opportunity. Not many QA nurses could say they had worked on the Medical Emergency Response Team and flown into the heat of battle to evacuate wounded soldiers. Two adrenaline filled shouts already in this twenty four hour duty. He was just sorry for Flight Sergeant Hughes, the RAF emergency nurse who was so ill with flu, and grateful to Major Breslow, the surgical Registrar for suggesting Scott as a suitable replacement. Like all other units, the hospital was starting to lose staff due to the drawdown and eventual handing over to the Afghans in 2014. With Scott's experience out on patrol with troops in Iraq and then in the early years of the Afghanistan conflict as a nurse in the Queen Alexandra's Royal Army Nursing Corps he was the ideal candidate until Andy got better. Scott had been taught life-saving skills normally performed by a doctor and some that few NHS nurses could only dream of doing. Besides, Major Breslow had an old score to settle. 'So, been on eBay lately?' the doctor enquired.

Scott chuckled. 'No telling Sir. You'll only try and outbid me!'

'Yes well, it should have been mine, fancy selling it?'

'No thanks Sir, but you are welcome to come and have a look at it. Though I have to warn you it's safely at home in Garthdee with my dad whose looking after my collection until I can afford to put down a deposit on a flat in Aldershot. My extra allowances for being out here and not being able to go out or shopping should help too. It'll be fine and handy for working at Frimley Park or 22 Field Hospital. I'm getting too old to be living in barracks.'

'Garthdee?' enquired Major Breslow.

'Aye Sir, the area in Aberdeen I'm fae.'

'Ah.' he acknowledged, still getting used to this strange dialect which Scott had been trying to teach him during this spell of stand-by. He couldn't help but smile at this likeable fellow and though he could understand *from* being *fae* he could not get his head around why a Scottish dialect was called Doric when it had nothing to do with Greek columns. Even Scott couldn't understand that. Though he was more interested in getting his hands on the Military Medal Scott had won on eBay. It was rare to see one with such history and provenance. It had belonged to a Nursing Sister in the QAIMNS, one of the few regulars out of 300 to be awarded the MM, though many of the Reserve, over ten thousand by the end of the Great War, had also been awarded them. He really wanted that for his collection. It was especially rare because in June 1916 King George V added an amendment to the Royal Warrant that women could be awarded it. This one at auction had been awarded just a few weeks later, the first ever for an army nurse. Normally families handed them down to each generation but he guessed this Sister had died with no next of kin or perhaps poverty had forced them to sell it. Normally they were handed down to Great Nieces and Nephews since few early QAs married because in those days they had to give up nursing to wed. The thoughts of the establishment were that a nurse could not devote herself to a husband and her patients. It was one or the other. Instead they selflessly dedicated their lives to nursing, though spoiling rotten their brothers' and sisters' children, growing close to them as surrogate children who doted on the heroic tales of their aunts. 'So what have you got your eye on now?'

'It's a fine example of the first issue of the World War One Silver War Badge Sir. The seller doesn't know much about it but he did include the number on the back of it, so I did a little investigating online at National Archives and discovered through War Office documents that it belonged to a Nursing Sister who was discharged from the British Expeditionary Force in 1916, having spent two years at the front. Though she was injured, when she returned home to Britain she re-enlisted to serve at the Cambridge Military Hospital in Aldershot. I guess her disablement was only severe enough to affect frontline duties. It's a pity that hospital is closed, I'd have loved to look around it; I believe the clock tower is quite some sight.'

'Fascinating, I've one of those from an RAMC Corporal, it's surprising how cheap they sell for, despite the sacrifices their original owners underwent. I never understand why families don't hang onto these things. They were only given out to those servicemen and women who had been honourably discharged due to injury, wounds or illness, so they definitely did their bit. What's the name of the Nursing Sister it belonged too? He nodded his thanks as Corporal Layton handed him a cup of steaming coffee. She rolled her eyes at Sharon, her RAF colleague who was quietly sat by them completing a crossword, as if to say *they're at it again, boring us rigid about how big their military memorabilia collections are. Why don't they just unzip their trousers, whip out their dicks and have a measuring contest!*

'You'll never believe the coincidence, but it belonged to the same lassie who won the Military Medal. It was Sister…'

Scott was interrupted by the sound of urgent pounding of boots from the nearby portakabin where the aircrew relaxed between shouts. All eyes of the medical team were focused on the nearby phone as they anticipated its ring. They knew from past experience that when the aircrew were scrambled and ran to their craft, that they would be next. All thoughts of their social conversation over coffee forgotten, they were focused purely on their important roles now.

Just then a klaxon sounded outside and the phone rang. It was immediately picked up by Corporal Judy Layton who listened attentively and said thank you as she hurriedly put down the receiver. She turned promptly to her colleagues, reaching for her gear at the same time, and simply said 'We're on! Cat B. Nahr-e Saraj.' Corporal Grey, Major Breslow, and her fellow Royal Air Force paramedic, Sergeant Sharon Massey, leapt to their feet and grabbed their personal body armour and helmets and quickly did their pistol checks. They swiftly put these on as they made their way to the army Land Rover that would speed them on their way from the MERT hut to the chinook. Though only a short distance, every second was precious. In the distance they could see the pilot and navigator already climbing into the cockpit and as the Land Rover pulled up to the tailgate the pre-flight checks were being performed. The Loadmaster ushered the medical and nursing team in just as the members of the RAF Regiment Force Protection Squadron pulled up and started to unload their weapons. These gunners provided covering fire when needed and all round protection of the Chinook in the event of Taliban snipers or insurgents, not spotted by the troops on the ground or the Apache helicopter pilots. Brigade HQ had already scrambled the Apache helicopters which were now in the skies above waiting to escort the MERT and their precious personnel into the battlefield.

Scott sat down in the back, he could never get used to the sudden darkness from the bright light outside. Though the Chinook had small windows they let in little light and internal lights were seldom used in case they attracted enemy fire. Instead there was a small green light to help with vision to perform their necessary tasks. As the Loadmaster counted the team in and spoke through his radio to the pilot, Scott put on his yellow ear defenders to protect against the noise. Though he would also plug into the intercom headphones he may have to take these off if he had to leave the aircraft to help load up casualties, or move around between patients, so he wanted to protect his ears from the deafening noises of the regular thump thump of the rotor blades and the heavy engines. The pilot would not turn them off after landing to save precious minutes so that the casualty could get back to Camp Bastion as soon as possible. This action also minimised the risk of enemy assault on the helicopter and its precious cargo of personnel. His eyes were protected by goggles, vital for the dust storm cloud that the large twin rotors would kick up along with debris and stones. He recalled one squaddie who hadn't tucked in his combat shirt into his trousers during uplift. He had sustained painful grazing which took weeks to heal, from the gravel travelling at such a velocity whipping into him like a frenzied ringmaster trying to tame a performing lion. He required a short course of antibiotics to prevent skin infection. Once the Loadmaster had accounted for all the team and their Force Protection Squadron he would radio through to the navigator and pilot and then they would be airborne and Scott and his colleagues could ready their medical equipment during the trip there, all while silently praying that no lucky Taliban struck at them with a Rocket Propelled Grenade launcher, though knowing the experienced Apache pilots could almost certainly see off any RPG attack. The medical equipment was always restocked after each shout as priority and just needed to be hooked up and placed in immediate reach. Scott ran through some plasma expander liquid and despite the movement of the helicopter ensured that no air bubbles were in the giving set. He attached this life saving plastic bottle to one of the special hooks dangling from the ceiling. He knew that HQ would already be informing the trauma team at the hospital of the casualty's blood group so that they could cross match and have ready blood for him from the laboratory's well stocked blood bank and even arrange for transfusions from willing volunteers around the base if more were needed. In the meantime they would use their stock of O Neg from the fridge since anyone could safely receive this.

Seldom did the nursing and medical team leave the relative safety of the helicopter, considered too valuable by military top brass and politicians because of their years of training and experience, to risk being shot at, the Taliban seeking Red Cross armbands and even women as highly prized targets. Though the RAF paramedics were permitted to leave the craft for handover. It was usual practice for the troops on the ground to bring the casualty up the tailgate, being signalled by the Medical Officer if the casualty was to be brought up head or feet first, depending on the injuries and the type of exit flight undertaken by the pilot. A nose take off could affect the blood flow of an already compromised casualty who had bled out vital fluids in the battlefield. Though the reality, which was not reported to the upper echelons, was that many a doctor and nurse had set foot on enemy land to help the paramedics and soldiers bring the maimed troops on board. Scott just prayed that the casualty would hold out, whilst secretly hoping that Naomi was safe wherever she was and maybe even their company medic so that he could get a rare sight of his fiancée. He missed her and ached to be with her. They hadn't seen each other since their last leave together in Aberdeen where his father eagerly awaited them. He and Naomi had bonded years ago over his beloved doos. Dad took immediately to Naomi, especially as she was so interested in his racing pigeons and his loft in the back garden. They seemed to bring her peace and the nightmares seemed less when she was at Dad's. She loved the way that they would pop back into the sputnik trap after a flight round the neighbourhood, their heads continually bobbing as they gently cooed as they made their way back into the shed. She even went with him to a racing meeting to see his girls and boys released with the others in the club. Dad won his first race when she first went with him and he considered it was because Naomi brought him luck and always asked after her during his calls home on Skype. He now tried to arrange races when she was home. He smiled briefly as he thought of his beautiful soul mate and wished he could hold her and feel her silken black hair and hold her close. He silently prayed for her safety too. Checks over, the others sat grim faced, not knowing what lay ahead, other than the information from the nine liner.

3

For the past 20 years she silently watched as her hospital emptied,

first of her charges, and then of the equipment, beds and furniture.

Still she remained silent and unobtrusive, never intervening,

knowing that one day she would once again care for tormented

souls, twisted in agony, grateful for the relief she could provide,

comforted by her presence and light touch. Even when the intruders

came with their handheld portable lights in one hand and strange

metal objects held up to eye level which scanned the long corridor

outside her ward, still she kept her silence. Though they broke

through her ward door and entered her domain she remained in the

shadows, resisting the temptation to bid them to leave, stifling her

anger and rage at their blatant intrusion. Her day would come soon.

Over a decade later new strangers came, with white and green

hard hats and bright yellow jackets that almost hypnotised her to be

drawn out of the depths of her silent vigil. They had no right here, in

her domain, but still she watched quietly for she knew he was

coming, the one who would draw her out from the dark and allow

her once more to wear her white muslin veil and scarlet cape with

pride.

These labourers brought with them noisy machinery and soon her kingdom was altered. Walls destroyed and floors ripped up and new foundations built. Her kingdom changed and with it her anger grew. He must come soon for the rage seethed within her, her thirst to nurse a tormented soul needed to be slaked. Scott, his name was Scott, and he was coming, and soon he would be hers.

'Wheels down in two minutes' announced the Loadmaster at the same time as giving the hand signal, above the full roar of the engines, to alert those not hooked up to the internal communications. This was especially important to the Gunners of the RAF Regiment who needed to be off the craft instantly, alert for any hostile activity, prepared to fight tooth and nail to protect the medical crew as the casualty and deceased was boarded. Their fingers ready to flick off their safety catches as they ran down the lowering tailgate, rifles raised to provide covering fire and eliminate any Taliban, each openly wanting to slot a raghead, hatred borne because of the high number of casualties they had seen over the months of their tour. All eyes remained on the Loadmaster, the true boss of the aircraft. Behind these eyes dark shadows lurked, nightmares ready to surface, of men who had seen too many battlefield victims being worked on during the flight home, impotent to help but marvelling at the dedication of the doctor and his team, calmly and proficiently they went about their care. Never before had they seen such trauma, loss of limbs, blood, exposed tissue and bone and each fervently hoped they would never again after this tour, though none had any regrets, and would not replace such sights unless it made fellow brothers-in-arms whole again.

The pilot and navigator simultaneously spotted the smoke signal that displayed their safe landing zone and quickly plotted a course, aware of the two Apache pilots to either side of them, and in constant radio communications as they swiftly moved around the area, seeking out activity using their top of the range thermal imaging equipment; ready to release a nightmare of artillery that included Hellfire missiles and a 30mm chain gun that would obliterate any enemy, leaving little to knock on the gates of Hades.

The MERT pilot subconsciously checked the area for any enemy activity, aware of the ground troops hunched down over their casualty, on the stretcher, with a body bag and kit on another, but out of his view. The soldiers were gathered in front of their fallen comrade, all but one facing outwards, rifles were at the ready. The other smaller soldier was holding the hand of the casualty, poking out of a groundsheet, whilst holding up a bag of solution. Her eye shield ready to protect her from the downdraft. The soldiers would quickly turn away from the downdraft to protect their faces, though still alert for the enemy. He knew that at this point the medic would reluctantly let go of the casualty's hand, not wanting her comfort to be withdrawn, but needing to protect the exposed flesh of her casualty from the sand, stones and muck that he would helplessly throw at them as she tucked it into the sheet. As always he would make sure he would go in fast and hard and not waste a precious second. As he effortlessly touched down with as much grace as this long trusted behemoth of the Royal Air Force could muster he alerted the Loadmaster and he and the navigator prepared for what he hoped would be a swift extraction and take-off.

'Go, go, go!' shouted the loadie above the roaring of the engines and whump whump of the rotors that remained turning, as he signalled for the Force Protection to exit. As they pounded down the lowering tailgate onto the hard Afghan terrain he signalled for the medical team to stay put. He had seen that there were enough boots on the ground to bring the injured and the dead on-board. He then made for the M60D machine gun, prepared to rain down 7.62mm calibre automatic rounds onto any enemy careless enough to expose themselves. He swivelled this killing beast on its mount, ready to unleash a mortal spree of up to 550 rounds per minute, all the time keeping a watchful count on his charges, along with his oppo on the side-mounted machine gun.

The RAF Regiment lads formed their protective arc, professionally ignoring the movement of the ground troops and stretchers, eyes only for enemy insurgents. Their arc of fire well exercised and second nature. Their Sergeant commanding his men through their own radios, once satisfied he signalled to the loadie that all was well. He in turn signalled to the medic, recognising her from her RAMC tactical recognition flash of maroon, blue and gold on her upper right arm of her jacket, no longer able to wear the Red Cross armband on her left arm which was now seen as too much of a tempting target for the Taliban who ignored any of the rules of the Geneva Convention regarding armed conflict. She was clutching a piece of paper that flapped furiously in this unnaturally made wind. He knew that this would be the treatment details of the casualty, which she would hand to the doctor since conversation was impossible due to the noise. The loadie had been informed by the pilot that it would be a nose down take off so the medical officer had decided on receiving the casualty head-first to try and maintain blood flow. This was signalled to the medic.

'Okay,' shouted Naomi to the three soldiers at the other handles of the stretcher, 'after three we'll lift and carry Billie in a steady walk to the helicopter, head first.' She waited till each nodded their understanding, wanting no sudden movements to cause Billie any undue pain or further blood loss or disturb his chest catheter. 'One, two, three lift.' yelled Naomi, above the roaring engines and rotor blades. Her drill Sergeant would have been proud of her loud commanding orders. As a team they made their way steadily to the tailgate, nodding to the loadie as they ascended the tailgate into the dimness of the MERT helicopter.

Scott's heart was racing. He recognised that beautiful figure, despite the blood stained, dirt covered combats and equipment. Even her helmet could not completely cover her luscious hair, though it could do with a good clean he thought as he grinned at her. He waited patiently not just to receive his casualty but to surprise his beloved Naomi.

As if perfectly choreographed the soldiers and Naomi placed down the stretcher of their team mate on the floor as signalled by the two RAF paramedics, each squaddie patting him softly on the shoulder and giving him the thumbs up before turning and running out of the craft to bring in the body of Ewan and Billie's kit, two stopping at the side of the huge aircraft to grab replacement stretchers. Scott discretely wrinkled his nose, the smell of the battlefield casualty carrying over to him despite the smell of aircraft fuel. It was a mixture of deeply unpleasant body odours, caked in mud, dirty uniforms and the unmistakable cloying aroma of fresh and drying blood. He had been warned by Corporal Layton to expect this. She told him it was one of the first things they learned at the MERT familiarisation course at RAF Brize Norton, even before they experienced and trained in the simulators and mock up scenarios. They often used real life amputees to make the scenarios more convincing. Sadly Scott never attended this course at the Tactical Medical Wing since he was never expected to be part of the team. He had experienced similar smells in Iraq and also back at the resus bay at Camp Bastion Hospital, though much of the smelling uniform had been removed by then, by the paramedics, nurses and even on occasion by the Gunners of the RAF Regiment during multiple casualty extractions.

Naomi, patted Billie lightly on the shoulder, he was able to look up at her and tried to lift an arm in farewell, but she knew he was too weak from blood loss and confused by morphine. She smiled at him nevertheless and stood up to look for the doctor and she was shocked to look straight into the grinning face of Scott. Overjoyed, she wanted to run into his arms and let him take her away from this ordeal, but had to remain professional. They were able to mouth *I love you!* to each other and exchange cheesy grins whilst the medical officer did some quick checks as the paramedics started hooking Billie up to oxygen, a cardiac monitor and pulse oximeter. Behind them Ewan's body was being reverently brought on-board. Major Breslow took the piece of paper out of Naomi's hand, reading quickly, he then gave her the signal that he was happy with the handover of the casualty. This was her cue to leave the aircraft and reluctantly she knew she had to leave Scott, but not before blowing him a loving kiss and he returned it with a wink whilst attaching the plasma drip to Billie's cannula. Having seen how shut down Billie's veins were and having no success inserting another cannula, Judy was already opening the EZ-10 intraosseous needle drill and infusion system. She would use this small drill to bore down into Billie's shoulder joint area where she could then insert the specialist needle into the humeral head to allow the paramedics to start his vital blood transfusion. The blood bank had fast tracked two units straight to the MERT helicopter as soon as Billie's zap number had been confirmed and his blood group established. They also had their stock of O Negative to fall back on, if needed, in their special fridge. More units of blood would be waiting at Camp Bastion Hospital. Major Breslow could also give Billie stronger drugs to better manage his pain, or deliver any other medicines, via Billie's bone marrow and straight into his bloodstream. Seeing Judy unzip the pack, he reached across for a packet of sterile gloves, to put over his already bloodied latex ones, and studied Billie's heart rhythm and vital signs on the monitors. He knew the risk of a cardiac incidence was imminent and that inserting a chest drain was his priority, Sharon was already checking the tourniquet and bandage and when cleared by her it would stay on until handover to the surgical team at Camp Bastion. She suspected that this would be a right turn resuscitation which meant that the casualty would go straight to the operating theatre rather than the normal resuscitation bay at this role three hospital.

Naomi ran to the tailgate, stopping briefly to grab a replacement battlefield trauma bag from the small equipment cache. Once she was back on Afghan soil she ran from the area to where the soldiers were hunkered down and positioned in defensive arcs. The loadie signalled to the RAF Regiment who returned swiftly to the craft, the Apache helicopters still hovering around the area, seeking out any tell-tale body heat. As the RAF Regiment Force Protection Squadron entered the aircraft once more, they took up their defensive positions, joining the loadie in pointing their weapons down the tailgate as the ramp started to rise and the helicopter tilted and rose in the air. Suddenly there was the sound of a roaring whoosh as the nearby compound exploded; a huge black mushroom cloud engulfed the air. Chunks of wall, wood and metal rained down on the Jocks, Naomi included, battering at their personal body armour and helmets. Scott looked up from his patient in disbelief as Naomi and her friends lay on the ground, pools of blood soaking into the soil. He stood up, reaching for his newly issued Glock 17 pistol, sliding back the breech to load a bullet into the chamber, moving instinctively to his beloved despite the turbulent movement of the helicopter that took part of the blast, the metal framework having taken a pounding by fallen debris from the compound. The other medical team were too busy working on Billie to notice Scott, each too shocked at the sudden blast noise and looking to the loadie, who was aiming his monster of a machine gun at the blast site, also unaware and stunned. He looked to the wounded squaddies, but knew that protocol dictated that the pilot would have no option but to return to Camp Bastion with immediate haste, the protection of the medical team and this casualty a top priority, whilst the Apache pilots searched fruitlessly for the enemy – all their sophisticated equipment could not have revealed the hidden timer on the ammo and weapons cache. All pilots radioing hastily in to HQ with an update so that another helicopter, probably their US equivalent with medical team, could be immediately scrambled. Scott made for the remaining battlefield trauma bag, but was knocked back as the helicopter tilted again, he fell roughly against the side of the craft, his helmet crushing into his ears, as it bounced against his skull, sounds muffling and ringing, causing him to become disorientated. He was knocked back to his left and fell hard against the floor, his skull taking the full impact, blood trickling out of his helmet, lying unconscious by the stunned gunners, as unmoving as the nine man team of the 4 Scots and Naomi.

4

Two Years Later.

Her war was supposed to be the war to end all wars. But it wasn't.

She was disheartened to witness the carnage of the Second World

War, the further loss of lives, limbs, sight, hearing and disablement.

She was further distressed as she saw the casualties come home from

the Korean War, Aden, Cyprus, the Suez Canal, Northern Ireland,

The Falkland Islands, where-ever that was, and Yugoslavia. She

proudly still did her bit and helped the souls find comfort into the

next life, helping to ease their passage to be with loved ones long

gone. When she was left alone and the wards emptied she kept

abreast of issues where her girls, and now boys, since men were

admitted to her beloved QAs from 1992, were posted to from

snippets of conversation between workmen and from reading their

newspapers, left after coffee breaks, or from news reports from loud

boxes which she had learned years ago were called radios. She

heard about the horrors of Kosovo and Bosnia, another Gulf War,

the first was bad enough when they temporarily closed her Kingdom

down from 1990 to 1991. Perhaps if this had never happened the

Politicians would never have fully shut down her domain in 1996.

51

She sighed, the asbestos could have been easily removed by specialist teams and once more her Kingdom could have provided the excellence of care it was renowned for. She still marvelled at the memory of working with Captain Gillies of the RAMC who pioneered plastic surgery on battle scarred soldiers. His facial surgery, adapted after watching French surgeon Hippolyte Morestin was life-changing for those brave men back from the Battle of the Somme. Even her beloved Hugh benefited from his diligent skills and those of dentist William Kelsey Fry. Ah happy days, she thought. She said a silent prayer for those Queen Alexandra's nurses serving in Sierra Leone that she lately read about over the shoulders of builders as they took a break from knocking down and transforming her Kingdom into flats. She was proud to read stories about the lives saved by medics, nurses and doctors. Though she thought she would never have another soul to help she stayed as all around her changed beyond recognition, except the clock tower, which remained untouched, though cleaned and repaired. It was like her temple, a place to pray and contemplate. To her it was a safe haven of calming refuge as all around her changed. She was powerless to stop the changes. She made her way there, as she did every day, as she had *every day since the accident which took her to Hugh, lovely darling*

Hugh. Though the top corridor had long gone, indeed the building

was much taller, to be replaced by what people in shiny suits called

executive flats, she found that her old feet still took her along this

route. She almost appeared to glide through the carpeted rooms. She

found her way to the entrance to the old wooden staircase to the

clock tower, where above she could look out and wait for Scott.

Scott exhaled long and slow, grateful that another day at the Ministry of Defence Hospital Unit in Frimley Park was over. Though he enjoyed being a wound care specialist, and was grateful for the Army in sending him on courses to achieve this new qualification, he wanted to get back into the thick of things. As he steered his car onto Queen's Avenue in Aldershot, to begin the long drive up to his flat, he pondered over the last few months. He knew he was lucky not to have been court-martialled over his intention to leave the MERT helicopter and try to reach the squaddies and save Naomi, pistol in one hand and battlefield trauma bag in the other. He felt inadequate that he never even made it off the craft, instead succumbing to a head trauma that left him with a small degree of brain injury. The months in Headley Court Rehabilitation Centre, learning to speak, walk and even look after himself in everyday simple tasks was made more bearable knowing that his beloved Naomi had survived the timer bomb, found under a pile of dead soldiers, injured, but still alive. Her presence in Headley made his frustrating time there more tolerable as he heard her badger him during each exercise to stick with it and retrain his brain in the simplest of tasks. She was the stronger of the two and despite her arm injuries she was always with him, even during his worst headaches and mood swings. Such a shame the building would soon no longer be used by servicemen and women, front line soldiers, like those Naomi now served with. They would instead benefit from the improved facilities being built at Stanford Hall. Life goes on, he thought, and now he had to look to the future with Naomi and start planning their wedding.

He turned left into Hospital Road, his eyes always attracted ahead to the magnificent clock tower. He felt an affinity with it somehow. He wasn't sure why, but even when leaving his flat for his nightly jog through the area, he would always find himself stopping to look up and admire the lit up dials and check his iPhone to see if it was keeping time. It always did, in perfect synchronicity. He could never explain why he was always drawn to it; perhaps it was the military connection. He still loved his army collection and memorabilia and was now focusing more on the QAIMNS side of things. He was continuing his research into the history of the old Cambridge Military Hospital, began during his long months at Headley Court, unable to explain to the Occupational Therapist why he wanted to learn more about this former army hospital. Just that he would often dream about it and wonder during the day what life was like over the decades for the patients and nursing staff. When he was discharged he had wanted his own space and couldn't believe his luck when a flat in the converted buildings of the old CMH was available to buy. He had saved up enough out in Afghanistan and whilst at Headley to put down a deposit. He knew it was almost like coming home, being somewhere that the older members of his Corps had nursed. He slept better here, though that may have had something to do with Naomi being by his side when she was off duty from 22 Field Hospital, grateful that she had survived Sierra Leone and not having contracted the Ebola virus when she went out to help run the hospital at Kerrytown. That was a long lonely time, but that's life in the army he grimly thought.

As he parked he sensed being watched, *probably just Naomi looking out for me*, he thought, *hope she's got a brew on*. He eagerly locked his car and walked to the flat complex main door, went through the spotless foyer, ignored the lift, and took the stairs two at a time, relishing the pumping warm feeling to his legs, knowing he had to get fitter if he was to be allowed to be posted back to a more exciting role than advising on and dressing wounds and day to day nursing. Headley physiotherapists and occupational therapists had healed his mind and to an extent his weakened body, but now it was up to him to get army fit again. The evidence of his MERT colleagues had saved his career and now he had a second chance and was not going to waste it.

'Fit like quine?' he cheekily shouted to Naomi as he unlocked his front door. He loved to tease her by speaking Doric.

She was now quite versed in this greeting of how are you girl? to which one day she had replied 'Aye, nae bad, foos yer doos ma loon?' surprising Scott with her put on broad dialect and use of a common phrase in rural Aberdeenshire. He knew where she had learned *how are you* and *how are your pigeons my boy* from. It could only have been from his father during her last leave home in Aberdeen, a well-deserved several weeks after the harrowing sights in Africa.

Scott always played the game and replied 'Aye Pecking Awa!' which meant he was well. He cuddled up to her, or as Aberdonians would say, he gave her a bosie. 'I love you sweetie!' he said, moving slightly back from the embrace so that he could look deep into her eyes.

'I love you too, there's a small package for you in the lobby, I haven't bothered picking it up yet.'

'Lazy cow!' joked Scott as he walked over to pick it up. It had lain beneath the letterbox and his entrance into the flat must have pushed it against the wall. His eyes lit up as he straightened up, 'I think it's the medal I bought last week from Sally Bosleys Badge Shop.'

Naomi rolled her eyes, not yet married and already a widow to his collection she thought fondly. Feigning interest she said; 'oh, let's have a look then.'

Scott eagerly peeled back the brown paper and was pushing his clumsy thumbs and fingers through the bubble wrap to reveal a silver medal that he held up by a blue, scarlet and white ribbon. Around the front face of the medal were the words Queen Alexandra's Imperial Military Nursing Service and in the centre was a cross with the letter A in its middle. 'It's an original,' he enthusiastically said to Naomi, 'not like the replica.' He pointed across to his display cabinet on the wall that they could just see from the open door to their bedroom. Scott walked across to it and opened its door. He removed the replica and placed it on his bedside cabinet.

'How much was that then moneybags?' asked Naomi, always keen to learn how much her daft fiancé paid for his hobby.

'Oh that,' pointing once more at the replica, 'only £20.'

'No not that you idiot, I know that was £20, I was there when you bought it at the medal shop in London. I'm talking about this new one?'

'Ah' replied a sheepish Scott, mumbling now 'not much, it's an investment really, one day, when I'm dead and gone and you and our children inherit my vast fortune it'll be worth a mint.' He leaned forward and ran his fingers through her black fringe, and then across to rub her neck gently, a habit he had got into whenever he wanted to placate her.

Not convinced, but enjoying the feeling of Scott gently massaging her Naomi looked across at it, where it now took pride of place in his cabinet alongside what she had learned several months ago was a Military Medal and a Wound Badge that Scott also called a World War One Silver Badge. 'What's so special about this one then?'

Scott became even more animated and took out the medal from the display cabinet and absently started to rub it, 'remember I was telling you about my research at National Archives and Keogh Museum?'

replied Scott referring to the Army Medical Services Museum in nearby Ash Vale. Naomi nodded, fearing another of his animated lectures on the history of the QAs. 'Well this one is an original that belonged to a Nursing Sister in what you'd maybe call the regular QAs, rather than the Reserve. There were only 300 but by the time of the Great War this leapt to over ten thousand nurses due to the number of wounded needing nursing care overseas and in Britain. They joined the Reserve. So to be able to buy an original is quite rare, they don't often come up for sale, especially not online. This one has the silver hallmark as 1912 on the back and you'll never believe this, but it belonged to the same Nursing Sister who owned these two,' said Scott pointing back to the cabinet.

'And who was she?' asked Naomi, starting to get more curious about Scott's passion.

'Sister...' began Scott, only to jump and drop the medal as a mug fell from the nearby kitchen and shattered loudly across the wall, spilling warm coffee over the cabinet fronts and pooling around the skirting boards as if trying to reach the photo higher up of Scott and Naomi taken at their engagement party.

5

Over the decades she had let slip to others her presence. It was little things that gave her away like her smell of lavender perfume as she walked past. Or the way it went cold to others whenever she was around, particularly in the top corridor or around those who lay dying. Throughout she resisted the temptation to reach out and make contact with fellow QAs. Her vigil was a lonely one, her role to comfort the dying, not to converse with the living. It did make her chuckle though when from the shadows she would watch the pupil and student nurses and the ward stewardesses and care assistants gingerly make their way around the hospital at night. It was always these youngsters who looked the most nervous, as if expecting her to jump out in her old fashioned uniform and say boo!

The older night sisters didn't give their nervousness away, but she knew that they and more experienced enrolled and staff nurses secretly feared her. Even the big burly medics and male nurses walked in fear of her. But never during the day, just at night, after dark, after the witching hour. Her haunting began, though of course she knew it to be her vigil, watching over those in need, once or twice slipping up as she comforted them, leading them to the light, her duty over and being seen by a shocked patient or nurse.

Never before though had she been able to move an object, to reach out and make contact with something solid. But she grew angry as she watched Scott and Naomi paw at her belongings. Her medals earned through a life devoted to nursing, two years at the frontline, first at No 2 General Hospital Le Havre in France then at No 2 Casualty Clearing Station at Bailleul. Despite the sleeplessness, backache from bending over to tend to casualties on low stretchers or beds, bombs raining down nearby and the constant work in wet damp conditions she only took a weeks home leave before her new posting to 24 General Hospital in Etaples until fatigue overcame her and nervousness warranted a rest. She earned her service badge; she did her bit and then some. Maud McCarthy, the Matron in Chief of the British Expeditionary Force France and Flanders, had initiated her recommendation for the Military Medal when she had refused to leave her patients during a particularly heavy bombardment.

After a few weeks rest back in Britain, and seeing that dear Hugh was recovering, she begged her Matron in Chief, Miss Ethel Hope

Becher, to be allowed back to serve in the QAs. Her experience was needed; the brave soldiers required her care. Her request was granted and once more she proudly wore her QAIMNS medal. This time she served on the Home Front, at the Cambridge Military Hospital in Aldershot, where her beloved Hugh was recuperating from wounds sustained at the Battle of Loos. The medal Scott had in his hand was hers. Now was the time to make her presence known...

Scott followed Naomi through to the kitchen, 'What the fuck!' she blurted out as she squatted by the broken cup. 'How on earth did that get all the way over there? I left it by the kettle; I'd only just made it for you as you came in.'

'No idea love, though I see you still swear like a trooper.' Scott was old fashioned and didn't like to hear a lady use foul language, especially one he planned to marry. He stooped to pick up the broken bits of the cup. He placed these in the swing bin and went into the cupboard for the mop. 'It's made a fair bit of mess though, let me clean up.'

'I've a better idea,' replied Naomi as she went to Scott, put her arms around him and kissed him softly on the lips, gently teasing him with her tongue and pulling playfully away as he became aroused, forgetting about the mess, focused purely on her. 'Let's go back to the bedroom, but not to see your new toys, I want to be your plaything now!'

Scott pulled her back, close to his body, where she felt his arousal hardening, he wrapped his arms around her waist and she jumped up to him, wrapping her legs around his buttocks, tightening them around, drawing him closer to her, kissing him more passionately. Scott responded by gripping her tightly, one arm around her buttocks, squeezing playfully, whilst in contrast lovingly running his fingers through her soft hair. He carried her through to the bedroom, stepping over the dropped medal, and placed her gently on the bed. She kicked off her trainers as she sat up to take off her t-shirt, exposing her breasts with hardened nipples. He knelt down by her and unbuttoned her jeans, pulling down her trousers and knickers in one practised movement, drawing in her special scent, wanting desperately to take off his own boxers and jeans which were hindering his erection. Scott ran his fingers slowly up her smooth legs, ignoring the scarred area where shrapnel from the bomb had painfully sliced into her, inching his way slowly to her loving area, where he gently stroked her as she gasped in delight, arching her back, bringing her vaginal area higher up to Scott who reached up and tenderly made his way up her body with his left hand, once again ignoring the scars, this time on her bare arms. Reaching her right breast he smoothly took it in his hand to caress, before reluctantly letting go and working his way around her nipple, to

65

finally take it between his fingers, giving it a gentle pull. Naomi groaned in ecstasy and breathlessly said: 'take off your clothes Scott, this is getting a bit one sided.'

Scott stood back and swiftly pulled off his sweater, unbuckling his belt, never taking his eyes of his beloved. She reached down to her clitoris and gently circled it with her middle finger. 'Hurry up; I might go off the boil!' Scott hastily removed his jeans, boxers and socks and was about to get back onto the bed. 'Mmm, wait a minute lover boy,' purred Naomi softly as she sat up and went to the edge of the bed, grasped his penis and started to masturbate Scott. It was his turn to gently moan with passion. He got louder as her strokes got faster and gasped as she ran her tongue up and down his shaft before taking him into her mouth, turning her spit around his penis as she moved her mouth up and down, looking playfully into his eyes, stopping and tightening her hand around his shaft as she felt him start to throb. 'Let's save this, I want you deep inside me,' she said as she lay back on the bed, starting to stroke her clitoris seductively again. Scott opened his bedside cabinet, fumbling for some lubricant and applied some to himself. He knelt once more on the bed, flipped Naomi over and as she went onto her knees he moved behind her.

Scott gave a contented sigh an hour later; he had fallen into a deep sleep, the peaceful kind achieved after exhaustive but satisfying love-making. 'Wow!' he declared as he reached across to Naomi but instead found his hand feeling amongst the sticky wet crumpled duvet. He shivered as he wondered where she was. Through the slightly open bedroom door he glimpsed a movement making its way quickly past the lobby, to the kitchen. 'Leave the mess sweetie, I'll clean it up, come back to bed for a doze.' Flicking the damp patch part of the duvet further away from him Scott got under the duvet and snuggled down. 'It's lovely and warm in here love, come back for a bosie.' He nuzzled into her pillow, enjoying the scent of her new perfume, and getting another stirring down below as he wondered if she was refreshed enough to enjoy more love-making. He was met with silence, not even the sound of mopping. He got out of bed and put on his dressing gown as he made his way through to the kitchen. There was no sign of Naomi, so he went through to the lounge, it felt chilly there, but there was still no sign of Naomi. He then made his way back to the lobby, to check out the bathroom, hoping to join her in the shower, he shivered again. He absently felt

67

the radiator and quickly removed his hand at its hot touch. *That's odd*, he thought, *its sae caul the day a Solicitor would walk doon Union Street wi his hands in his ain pooches*! He grinned; he must remember to tell that Doric joke to Naomi one cold day. The grin was wiped off his face as he walked into the empty bathroom. Getting worried now he quickly retraced his steps, a cold sweat forming around his body. His semi-arousal was now gone to be replaced with a tightening feeling around his balls and stomach. The knot of fear a soldier patient had once told him, always present when out on patrol, ready to face the worst. He panicked now as he saw the security chain still in place on the front door, *but where was Naomi*? he anxiously thought. He shook again with the cold, but perhaps also in fear for Naomi or a nagging doubt that his head injury from Afghanistan was once more causing his hallucinations. *But she must be in the flat, there's no other exit and he could smell new perfume* he thought. He sensed a sudden movement in the bedroom. *Ah*, he silently thought *she's playing games, but I'm onto her, her scent is giving her away*. He went into stealth mode, remembering exercises from his basic training at the Army Training Regiment in Winchester, long before he was blessed with knowing

Naomi. He silently made his way to the bedroom where a grey shadow was moving slowly up and down the wall, as if trying to suppress laughter. He reached to the door, steadying his breathing so that Naomi wouldn't be alerted to his presence and quickly opened the door, shouting 'Boo!' He went pale and felt dizzy from the heavy aroma of lavender as he looked straight into a skull set in a rictus grin wearing a veil and scarlet cape as a bony hand reached out menacingly for his throat.

6

Only once before had the rage inside her manifested itself to another. He was nasty, had no right being in the medical profession, unlike Scott who she sensed was a caring nurse. It was just after her beloved Hugh died and she briefly joined him before starting her vigils. It was the Royal Army Medical Corps orderly and Wardmaster who took Hugh down to the mortuary on the hospital cart. She had been able to watch this Sergeant Browning wheel him out of the end day room, down the ramp and along the path at the back of her hospital, lit by his swinging lantern, her poor Hugh draped in a sheet, flapping in the soft breeze. As Sergeant Browning wheeled Hugh down the steep hill, towards the lonely building, out of sight from the living, she feared he would fall off the cart. Instead his one remaining foot thudded into the wooden lipped edge of the cart, making a loud macabre thud of bone on wood to which this evil man just chortled and continued his merry whistling as he pushed her beloved onwards. But in this new form she was able to follow, her earthly body not yet found. The hospital was silent, the living patients asleep at this time, the dead about to have a new body to keep them company in their chilly room. It was a strange feeling being able to walk behind this horrible man, no sound emanating

from her shoes, she reached out her hand, curious at its grey pallor,

taking comfort that in this new form she was permitted by the higher

being to retain her cherished uniform.

Sergeant Browning halted the cart by banging it against the solid

oak door of the mortuary, again breaking the silence of the night

with his monstrous laugh. How she hated this sound that had no

place beside the cooling heat of her Hugh, his spirit long gone, but

spiritually still her lover and best friend. The evil man, still

chuckling away, unlocked the heavy padlock and slid back the bolt,

thudding it all the way back, breaking the silence of this solemn

event once more. Tree branches brushed against the roof of the

building as if welcoming in their new visitor, drawing him in. He

pulled open the creaky door and taking the lantern from the cart

went up the ramp and through the Chapel of Rest with its ornate

tiling depicting a scene of heavenly ascension from the bible and

table with velvet drapes. From the little moonlight that filtered

through the stained glass windows of Virgin Mary and Baby Jesus

she saw the carved words of scripture on the oak panelling above

which read 'I am the resurrection and the life', drawing comfort that dear Hugh was no longer in pain and in a better place. She followed Sergeant Browning through to the post mortem room, with its long silver tray that sloped slightly with the large angled tap at the other end and drip tray by the side, knowing that Hugh's flesh and bones would be indignantly cut in a few hours. She watched as he went into the other room as he counted out the other corpses, three poor souls who made the journey to heaven alone and possibly afraid until a loved one beckoned them on. 'Well no more,' she thought 'now these lost souls would have me.' She watched aghast as this medical orderly, who had risen to the esteemed rank of Wardmaster, a supposedly trusted position, began to check the hands of the corpses under the sheets and carelessly dropped their lifeless fingers back onto the trolleys. She knew what he was doing now, her suspicions about this man had been right all along, in life she suspected him to be a thief, a rotten apple amongst such a bunch of dedicated orderlies, working hard and so helpful to her fellow QAs, their mutual goal striving to keep patients comfortable, well and safe. She seethed and followed him back to what was left of Hugh, out in the cold night.

The Wardmaster pushed Hugh on his cart into the mortuary, through the Chapel of Rest which would not be needed since his family were in Aberdeenshire and would not be able to make the long train journey before he began to decay. She hoped his body would be laid to rest in his beloved city and not in nearby Brookwood Cemetery amongst the war dead. Not because he was ashamed of his service, far from it, he had proudly charged with his Battalion, the 8th Gordon Highlanders, over the top at the Battle of Loos, where he distinguished himself despite such odds. Rather she hoped his Regiment would dig deep into company funds and bring him home to his beloved Scotland where he could rest in peace. Unlike now where she looked in disgust as the Wardmaster heaved and humped dear Hugh by the shoulders onto the cold metal post mortem table, dropping his body with a clang as he made his way to the other end of the cart to slide across Hugh's remaining bluing leg and stumped thigh. These he swiftly threw across, Hugh's ankle bone bouncing twice off the metal in sharp contrast to the soft thump of his bandaged right stump high up his thigh. Her rage seethed and finally manifested itself, shocking her in its intensity as she ran, almost seeming to just propel her forward to Sergeant Browning, lips snarling, biting her lip until blood dropped between her lips,

turning her teeth and gums as scarlet as her tippet. As Sergeant

Browning made his way to Hugh's left hand, where he had

previously noticed the gold signet ring as the nurses were finishing

the last offices, he was aware of a sudden draft. Too upset by the

reaction of their colleague over this man's death they had omitted to

remove it, but he would, and a pretty price he would get for it too. As

he lifted the cold hand he was aware of a shadow by his side, a

freezing coldness and as he turned he dropped the hand in horror as

he saw a ghostly figure of a nursing sister, reaching out for him,

snarling with exposed bloodied teeth, saliva flicking across his face,

her eyes afire in hatred and screaming, 'LEAVE HIM!' He screamed

and fled the room, forgetting about his cart and not stopping to lock

the doors, desperate to distance himself from this horror. All

thoughts of riches far from his confused mind as he wet himself and

felt his bowels loosen with each pounding step into the dark windy

night.

'Scott, Scott, can you hear me? 'cried a worried Naomi who had found a pale looking Scott slumped in the doorway of their bedroom. She gently patted his shoulders as she asked him again, not wanting to move him in case he had hurt himself as he fell against the wall. He gave a groan as he came to, 'Don't move just yet darling, you've had another of your dizzy spells.' She looked to see if his dressing gown was wet, a sign that he may have had another fit. Thankfully it was dry, his last fit was over a year ago and he'd only just got permission from the doctors to drive again. 'Have you got your balance?'

Scott slowly nodded, a headache starting to form at the side of his skull. 'I think I banged my head on the way down, Christ, but that was an awful trick to play, I got the fright of my life,' he croaked as he rubbed his sore throat.

'What do you mean Scott, I just found you here; it was me that got the shock of her life!'

'Aye right, I guess that wasn't you moving the skeleton and hand, nice touch that dressing it in a scarlet tippet, I even noticed the medal on the right breast, glad you've been paying attention to our

75

conversations and put it on the correct side. Where have you hidden it and how did you hide yourself, I searched everywhere?'

'I've no idea what you are on about Scott, are you saying you saw something as you fell, another hallucination. Shit, I thought you were getting better,' she replied taking his hand and rubbing it gently, hoping he wasn't about to go into another rant, like those at Headley, before he was taught how to control them.

Scott focused his painful eyes on Naomi, the backs starting to hurt and could tell she wasn't kidding around, she never could tell a lie successfully, her twinkling eyes and upturned smile always giving her away. He usually won their card games. 'For real?' he implored.

'Yes Scott, for real. I've been making us a brew; after all that lovely activity I thought you'd be thirsty, especially as you didn't get the first one I made. I didn't realise how tired you were, I thought you were on the mend finally. Have you fainted recently?'

'No, this is the first time since sick leave after Headley, and I'm starting to get another of my famous cluster headaches.'

Naomi sighed, remembering how these had caused intense pain to Scott and made him crawl into bed and forget about the world, days would be lost. She had hoped they'd make a fresh start here in their

76

flat in Aldershot; with no medical problems to hinder their social life. The hallucinations after his head injury on the helicopter had been frightening enough at Camp Bastion Hospital that he had to be sedated for the aero-med flight home to Selly Oak Hospital in Birmingham, missing out on his decompression leave, carefully timed with hers, in Cyprus. Not that she'd enjoyed sunny Cyprus either, given her injuries. She admitted to being quite scared at some of his hallucinations, a drummer boy beating time to the marching troops into battle with Napoleon, skeletal men dressed in rags begging for food and freedom, piles of emaciated corpses rotting in a field; each so vivid to Scott that he could describe details, smells and sights. They still gave her the shivers, but this one sounded like he'd finally gone over the edge, one moment enjoying a post coital snooze, the next the horror of a nurse skeleton. 'Have you hurt yourself anywhere?' Scott shook his head, instantly regretting it as a fresh wave of pain and nausea swept over him. 'Let's get you back to bed – too sleep this time Romeo!' said Naomi as she put her arms under his right arm as he used his left to push himself off the floor where he indignantly lay, dressing gown flapping, revealing his glory. Naomi couldn't resist a cheeky look, smiled and said 'Okay

77

big boy, get your breath and walk over to the bed.' Scott gingerly took the few steps over to the bed and let out a big breath as he sat down, his head pounding and throbbing. Putting his head onto the pillow as Naomi tucked the duvet over him, the lubricant tube falling to the floor. He was soon peacefully asleep.

Scott awoke several hours later sensing movement by the doorway. His lips were dry and he hoped that Naomi was bringing him a fresh cup of coffee or glass of water. He needed to take some painkillers, but didn't want to risk moving his head without the safety net of someone being there to hand things to him because he was worried that a fresh wave of pain or gut sickening nausea would well up and force him to drop hot liquid. When he got like this he lost all sense of time, hours could seem like days whilst minutes could tick by and feel like hours. If left alone he could easily overdose on his codeine tablets, accidentally taking too many, further worsening tiredness and hallucinations. But was it an hallucination? He could still vividly recall the skeleton, not just dressed in a scarlet cape, but wearing a floppy white veil that stretched down her spine until those bones disappeared into a grey dress, with thick black stockings. Was he so

78

much into his hobby that he imagined the owner coming back from the dead for her property, angry at his ownership of them? Or perhaps he had returned to work too quickly, eager to please Major Dunn, the Nursing Officer In Charge of the Military Unit at Frimley Park Hospital, a lovely old man, who combined his natural air of authority whilst drawing out an eagerness to please from his subordinates. A true leader and one of the few QAs to have trained as a staff nurse within the army in the old Army School of Nursing and risen from the ranks and nursed worldwide in an assortment of military hospitals and field units, including Bosnia and the First Gulf War. During his induction interview he had regaled Scott with tales of his time as a Lance Corporal at the Cambridge Military Hospital and the pranks they had played on each other. His favourite had been the tale of dressing a drip stand in a spare uniform of one of the staff nurses or sisters and taping down the frilly hat or starched veil to the top and pulling it along adjoining ward entrances with string as one of the ward stewardesses was going along the low lit top corridor on a made up errand. He laughed along with the Major's reminiscences and then had to ask what a Ward Stewardess was. He learned that it was an early role for the current Health Care Assistants, not as

79

highly trained as they were now, but still taught basic nursing care and tasked to help keep the wards running smoothly by keeping equipment and stock levels high and assisting with meals and taking patient observations of pulse, temperature and blood pressure. The Major loved the questions about the old CMH that Scott kept asking during his interview and the weeks since and in turn Scott had learned so much about the old building where he now lived. He began to wonder if it had all been too much for him and that his brain had unconsciously dreamed up a vision.

His thoughts turned back to the present and the scratching noises he could now hear. It was almost as if a rat was trying to get through the door. There they were again, a clawing and scratching as if on glass. Now they were getting louder, a regular drumming beat as if against a window pane, talons scratching slowly but steadily down the glass. He felt the need to sit up and look around, but knew that he must calm himself and rise slowly to look so as to avoid vomiting as he previously had when he suffered these cluster headaches. Instead he slowly opened one eye which widened in horror as he saw the bony figure again, dressed in the old fashioned nursing uniform clawing at his medal cabinet on the far wall. Ignoring any pain he sat bolt upright, in cold shock and fear for he knew that there was no way Naomi could be playing a practical joke. The figure's legs seemed to be going down through the floorboards, but yet it could turn and stare at him without the carpet moving. It twisted grotesquely towards him, elongated taloned finger bones at once removing themselves from its fruitless attempts to open the cabinet and pointed them towards his throat as it appeared to glide steadily towards Scott. He jumped back on his bed, hitting his back against the headboard which in turn knocked against the wall; a noise he hoped would bring Naomi through. He tightening his dressing gown around his front in an attempt to draw comfort and pad out his throat from those talons. As she made her way to him he felt an odd tightening sensation in his groin and stomach as if he needed to urgently go to the toilet, knowing if he got there he would not be able to void, not responsible for his own natural actions. He felt rooted to the spot, mesmerised by those empty eye sockets which drew nearer and nearer until he once more felt the cold white hand bones around his throat and sunk once more into a dreamless state, his last sensation being the heady smell of lavender.

7

Over the decades she had listened into the conversations of her
fellow QAs and RAMC nurses and medics, sometimes even doctors.
Always at night; she was never mentioned during the day. The young
nurses would sit eagerly in their grey dresses and plain hats, hair
perfectly tied back in buns, or white tunics and trousers with
polished black shoes for the men, listening to the older much wiser
staff nurses with their red belts and frilly hats and sleeve cuffs. She
would hear their hushed almost reverent tones as they mentioned her
name. Well not by her birth name, the one proudly chosen by her
mother and father, the surname that died with them and her, for they
had no other children, but by the mysterious title of The Grey Lady.
Soon she came to forget her name, never hearing it for years, almost
a century; answering only to her new title. But she would never
forget her Hugh, his name constantly on her lips, hoping one day to
be with him again. Whenever the name of The Grey Lady was said
tales would be spoken. She always listened into these, hoping to hear
her name spoken aloud once more. To catch an acknowledgment of
her past service and her continued commitment to dying patients. It
never happened and she bitterly knew that it never would. She did

enjoy the enthusiastic way that the hospital staff tried to out-spook

each other with their theories and rumours of who she was and why

she died. Some even hiding in the dark shadows, awaiting an

innocent young ward stewardess, pupil or student nurse to walk past

so that they could jump out and scare them. Little did these enrolled

and staff nurses know that all the time she was with them in the dark

shadows, watching, keeping vigil. Many thought that she had killed

herself, thrown herself off the top floor balcony at the news that her

lover had been killed in action in France during World War One.

Others said her legend was that she was a dedicated nursing sister

who had accidentally given a patient an overdose of morphine which

led to his death and that overcome with guilt she had thrown herself

off the roof of the Cambridge Military Hospital and that now, in

death, she walked the dark lonely corridors helping the dead to

reach heaven. If only they knew the truth. It was too late for the staff,

long gone, the doors closed to patients on the 2nd February 1996, to

learn the facts, and too late for her to be a caring ghost once again,

with no lost souls to help pass over, but Scott would soon learn the

truth and be saved. She decided to reveal herself and complete one

more deed.

Scott awakened from his faint against the headboard, to feel the grip of the long bony hands weakening, he lethargically raised his head and as his vision cleared he could see maggots squirming in the eye sockets of the skull by his face. There was the cloying overpowering smell of decaying flesh, making him gag, wanting urgently to vomit. Several maggots fell out and dropped down his dressing gown front along with small pieces of rotting meat, he could feel them wiggling about his chest, still trying to feast on these tiny morsels of dead flesh, tickling against his hair. Scott wanted to move but was mesmerised at the sight of the skull which appeared to be growing flesh, nerves, capillaries and veins before him, meshing the fibres of the dermis, tightening up around the skull. Skin formed around these, enclosed the maggots, forcing them to stop their wiggling, bone and flesh no longer exposed, a tight protective shield of epidermis grew. The eye sockets became white, staring deep into Scott's soul as if trying to reach into his inner being and grab him from his very depth. They finally let go as a bright glassy blueness was woven, drawing him closer to this spirit. The horror was turning into beauty as before him brown hair rooted out of a newly formed skull, weaved itself into the veil which became whiter. He looked down to see whatever this was reach out her hands, only this time to place them gently in front of her newly formed eyes, as if seeing her fingers for the first time. She stretched them out and turned them over. Scott was also able to see the scarlet bands around both sleeves of her grey dress. Despite his fear he knew they signified her rank as Nursing Sister. *Good, God*, he thought, *this surely cannot be the grey lady, after all these years*? His testicles tightened again and he felt the knot of fear in his stomach churn, 'There's no such thing as ghosts,' he shouted, looking at her scarlet cape as it wrinkled with her movement, her medal bouncing off her right breast. She merely turned her attention away from her now formed hands and with her newly fashioned body moved back, inclined her head and walked to the medal cabinet. She pointed her pale fingers at them and moved towards them and straight through the wall.

Naomi burst through the door. 'What's all the shouting Scott, are you okay?'

'Did you see her, did she walk past you?' shouted Scott.

'Calm down, stop shouting, what are you on about?' asked Naomi as she sat on the bed, a look of deep concern furrowing her brow.

'Her, she was here again. I thought the first time was you playing tricks, but it wasn't was it? Then she appeared again, God but it was awful, she looked like a skeleton trying to strangle the life out of me one minute and then the next there's maggots, decayed flesh and then new flesh and skin formed around her bones. She looked straight into me Naomi, right into my soul, I'm sure she could feel what I was feeling. She knew me.' Scott began to gently sob and Naomi reached across to comfort him, pulling him to her chest, leaving him to cry for a few minutes. Her t-shirt started to feel wet, so gently moving her body away from him she pointed across to the bedside cabinet to the box of tissues 'Blow your nose and wipe your eyes, you've snotted over me!'

'Sorry,' replied a sheepish Scott as he reached over, took one from the box and patted his eyes with it before blowing his nose, 'I just don't understand what's happening. Am I going crazy, seeing things again, or am I being haunted? I don't mind telling you that I'm bloody scared.'

Naomi took his hand, 'Don't be daft, there's no such thing as ghosts. And stop swearing, you're always telling me off enough for that. You are just run down, tired and emotional. New job, new flat, great sex! You just need something to eat and drink and then back to bed for a good night's sleep,' replied Naomi trying to convince Scott and herself that all was well. Who could she report this to; clearly Scott was becoming unwell again, if only there was someone who would listen to her. She pointed over to the pile of clothes that he had earlier discarded in his rush to make love. 'Put those on, and go and get yourself something to eat and drink, then back to bed with you,' she coaxed while gently rubbing his hand.

Scott reluctantly removed her hand, giving it a fond pat, more to reassure him than her, then got up, removed his dressing gown, checking it for maggots, seeing none he gave it a shake, then shrugged and draped it over the bed and got dressed. As he walked out of the bedroom he looked at the display cabinet, glass still intact, and tapped on the walls, half expecting a false door to open and let him through. He gently shook his head, noting that his headache had gone. Perhaps I took too many codeine again he absently thought as he made his way to the kitchen, the last time that happened I had such vivid dreams. Here he stepped over the dried coffee stains, making a mental note to mop whilst his dinner cooked. Not feeling up to making an extravagant meal for Naomi and himself he opened the cupboard, took out a tin of baked beans and peeled back the easy to open ring pull. He emptied the contents into a saucepan, placed it on the electric ring and switched it to high. He then reached across to the breadbin. 'How many bits of toast do you want Naomi?' Not getting a reply he automatically slotted two into the toaster, pushing down the switch that started the gentle hum of the electrics browning his bread. He then set out two plates, two knives and two forks and placed these on the table just as the doorbell rang. Scott made his way to the door and as he absently took off the chain he wondered who it could be since he hadn't got round to giving out his address to anyone except at work. He opened the door to find a smiling middle aged man with a mop of unruly hair holding a box of chocolates. 'Padre!' exclaimed Scott, 'What are you doing here?'

'Hello lad,' replied Padre Caldwell, in his uplifting voice that always sounded like he was shouting, 'thought I'd see how your first day back at work was. These are for you,' he boomed, his voice carrying down the communal corridor, as he thrust the chocolates into Scott's hands. 'I never know what to get chaps, ladies are so much easier to shop for, flowers, you can never go wrong with flowers. Got the kettle on?' Scott smiled remembering how much tea the Padre had got through whenever he saw him on his shifts at Camp Bastion Hospital, working on the wards before his head injury. The Padre would spend hours with the wounded and sick servicemen and women, never a word about God, just lots of tea and chat, and plenty of games of dominoes. His calming presence working wonders for their spirits. 'Two sugars in mine please,' he requested as he made his way inside, shrugging off his coat and scarf as he followed Scott into the kitchen. He placed them on the back of the chair at the table. 'Ah sorry, interrupting your tea, oh I love baked beans on toast. My dear old mum used to grate some cheese on top of mine. It tasty lovely when it melted in and went all gooey, filled up my tummy too.' A puzzled look came over the Padre's face as he saw the two plates and cutlery. 'Already got company?'

'No, no Padre, please join me, the toast's just done. I haven't much of an appetite, please share it with me,' replied Scott as he took out the toast from the toaster, placed a slice onto each plate, turned off the cooker and spooned on the beans. 'No cheese though I'm afraid.'

'Not to worry, this is such a treat. The Mess food is alright, but this Yorkshire lad would prefer simple home-cooked meals any day of the week. Clasping his hands he bowed his head and said 'Shall we?'

Not waiting for a reply he quickly said a prayer of thanks and tucked

into his meal. 'So how was your day today? I popped into your unit

and they kindly gave me your address, knew you wouldn't mind.'

'Really eventful!' replied Scott unsure if he should tell the Chaplain

about seeing ghosts. 'I chatted with Major Dunn today, he's a good

laugh. He told me all about the history of the CMH during work.'

'Ah yes, lovely building, shame it had to be pulled down, though I

love that they've retained the clock tower. Nice bit of history, shame

the bells are no longer up there, I'd have loved to have heard them

chime. You cannot beat the wonderful sound of church bells nor

those in old clock towers. I never served here, closed before my

time, though I have heard stories over the years. I've seen some

impressive looking pictures of it on the QARANC website.'

'Oh aye?' prompted Scott.

'Yes, silly superstitious lot you army nurses. Supposed to be

haunted by a grey lady ghost, threw herself off the building when her

fiancé died. Back during the Great War. She got the blame for any

odd things that happened. Lost the drug trolley keys – blame it on

the grey lady. Cold draft – oohhh it's the grey lady come for avisit!

Course my Church's official line is that they don't believe in anything supernatural, though I've seen odd things in my life that between you and me have made my hair stand on end,' he ruffled up his hair resulting in it looking even more dishevelled, but still giving him an air of charm. 'I wouldn't tell my superiors about these odd occurrences though. They might take me away in a straight-jacket and throw away the key! And not before time some might say! Once, in my old village parish, a couple from the congregation came to the church. I'd never seen them before and I'd been there for several years before I got the calling to join the Royal Army Chaplains Department. Anyway they were really nervous and the wife in particular looked ill, like she had cancer, you know that pale, thin look, like they've been through so much and not knowing how much more they can take. Especially around the eyes, they were sunken and the skin around them so dark and grey. I had the sense that they had come to see me for a special reason but couldn't quite summon up the courage to ask me something. It was definitely more than someone who never comes to church about to ask the vicar if he would baptise their baby.' The Padre stopped his story to eat more of his baked beans on toast, between mouthfuls there were several 'mmms' as he evidently took great relish in this rare but simple treat.

In his mind he was thinking of his dear old mum and a fond smile appeared on his face.

Scott grew impatient, he wanted to blurt out his experiences and get help from the Padre, but knew it would affect his career so he refrained. Instead he joined in eating, though his appetite was lost, his mind still dwelling on his supernatural experiences.

'Yes,' continued the Padre, stopping to lick his lips. 'It turned out that their old Victorian house was haunted. The husband used the basement, the old servant's quarters, as his study. As the wife crossed the landing upstairs on her way to the kitchen one evening she saw a slim young lady, dressed in black enter his room. So she went rushing downstairs thinking that he had slipped in a fancy woman via the basement outside door. He had his headphones on and was busy typing up a work project whilst listening to some music. She looked around his room and of course he was unaware that his wife was there and got the fright of his life when she loomed over him to check under his desk thinking his new love was hiding from her. So of course he thinks his wife imagined it, but it kept happening, each evening he would go to his study to do extra work, it seems he was after a promotion, so this project was vital. And each

93

evening his wife would come bursting in looking for the young woman dressed in black.'

'Did the husband ever see the woman?' interrupted Scott. The Padre used the time to tuck into his surprise meal, never one to ignore or turn down a meal.

'No; never. In fact he told me that he had to take his wife to the doctor because he thought she was hallucinating. But she was medically well, though had been losing weight rapidly between consultations. The doctor tried every test and thought of different causes for these sightings that only the wife witnessed. She even had a psychiatric assessment to see if she was barking mad. She proved as sane as you and I.' The Padre looked up at Scott, with a cheeky grin, 'That is assuming we are both quite sane, the jury is still out on my decision! But do eat some more of your meal Scott, here's me gulping down mine and you've barely touched yours.'

Scott picked up his fork and toyed with his food. 'Continue the story Padre. I'd love to know what happened. I'll eat this up and listen.'

'Yes, well, the husband finished his project but sadly it wasn't good enough to gain him his much yearned for promotion. But I don't

94

think this really bothered him, because he could see how ill his wife was getting. Apparently the young woman could now be seen around the rest of the house. The wife saw her from the front and described her as wearing a white frilly pinny uniform over her black dress. This set off something in the husband's memory so he went exploring on the computer and typed his address into various search engines. By this stage his wife was really ill, her hair had lost its shine, she looked gaunt, wouldn't eat, couldn't sleep, you know all the signs of stress being a nurse Scott.'

Scott nodded as he looked at his empty fork. He was experiencing them himself at the moment.

'So to cut a long story short the husband found out that a maid had killed herself because she was accused by the lady of the house of stealing a necklace. A week after her suicide the necklace was found, it had fallen under the dressing table. The room was being redecorated and workmen, moving the heavy furniture had found it. Local gossip around the village tells the legend that in death the maid remains in the house, cleaning as a penance for a crime she knows she didn't commit. It seems the lady of the house took the necklace from the workmen and not a word was said. The maid had travelled from outside the community for her position so word never got back to her distraught parents. They died thinking she was a common thief, a big scandal in those times. With no other children the disgrace was soon forgotten in their village.'

'That's not right Padre, the poor wee lassie, so do you think her restless spirit still walks the house seeking the necklace?'

'Yes indeed, though as I say, my church would not officially acknowledge such a theory, nor sanction what I did.'

'Blimey, what did you do,' asked Scott, intrigued to learn how the Padre helped the couple and perhaps how he may also help him with these Grey Lady sightings.

'Alright Scott, but again I must stress the between you and me bit before I continue,' asked the Padre earnestly seeking Scott's consent.

Scott eagerly nodded his head in agreement.

'Well it was the husband who said it to me. And remember he was a sensible executive type. Though he lost out on this current promotion he was still highly placed in his organisation in the city. So he wouldn't come out with daft supernatural theories. He reminded me that he'd never seen the ghostly figure but did believe his wife. He would talk loudly around the house to the spirit, begging her to leave his wife alone, to leave this earth and find peace. He told her over and over again that she was not a thief and that the necklace had been found. He even got his wife to do the same, thinking that if the ghost heard it from the current lady of the house then the spirit would rest. But it didn't work and he came to me to see if I would do an exorcism.'

'Wow, does the church do that, I mean I've seen the films.'

The Padre laughed. 'No it's nothing like those horror films. No swivelling head and fountains of vomit. Ha ha, I'd run a mile if that happened! Nor does the church officially sanction exorcisms. But I did go to their house to say blessings and prayers with the couple, nothing unusual about that. I was simply a vicar bringing comfort to a fraught couple. I did feel a presence though Scott, you know when you feel the back of the neck hairs stand on end and a shiver down your spine, just like in the films or when you watch ghost films, I love watching those. Yes indeed, I went quite cold, though it was a warm summer's evening.'

'So what did you do?' Asked Scott impatiently, dying to hear how he really helped the haunted wife.

'This is for your ears only mind my boy.' The Padre looked earnestly at Scott who was nodding his head vigorously. Seeing his nod of assent he continued with his ghostly tale. 'I could see the wife was deteriorating between visits to the church and mine to the house. So one night I held vigil, with the husband and wife, I prayed silently and aloud with the couple. Then I lit a candle, prayed aloud to the ghost that she was innocent, that no-one now blamed her, especially the lady of the house, and that I was a man of the cloth and that God knew of her innocence and that he would welcome her to heaven with loving open arms. I told her that many years had passed and that her mother and father were waiting for her on the other side, in heaven.'

'And did she appear?' asked Scott, once more interrupting in his eagerness to hear the end of the story. *This Padre can really stretch out a story; no wonder the patients in Afghanistan loved his visits. It took away their boredom and transported them into other places as they listened to his tales* he thought with amusement. 'Did you see her?' he gushed out.

'No, nothing exciting such as an appearance to all of us and a walk by a saved spirit to bright lights with harps played by angels on clouds, just silence. So I packed up, they made me a cup of tea and I got a piece of the most moist and tasty carrot cake I have ever tasted and then I asked the couple to phone me in the morning and keep me updated over the coming weeks. I'm happy to say that the ghost or spirit or whatever it was stopped haunting the wife. She never saw the young girl again. The wife's health rapidly improved and became her beautiful happy self again. And I proudly converted two parishioners into regular church goers. She even sings in the choir each week. Best of all; and this is rather selfish of me but you know how much I love my food, she would bring me a different cake each week. She was so grateful to me and,' he paused to pat his stomach with affection, 'was single handedly responsible for this weight gain! The husband even got promoted the following year and they moved away because of the new job. Lovely couple, I baptised both of their children; I do miss them and her cakes. The power of prayer can sometimes be more powerful than pills and even the best of nursing care. I'm sure you've witnessed that Scott.'

'Aye, I have Padre, some patients who seem terminal, often survive to live months and even years longer than doctors predict. Perhaps it's their mind-set, a positive outlook that helps them get up in the morning and keep going. I've always loved the sense of community that churches bring and how friendly most are, perhaps that's another reason the power of prayer works so well. Er, so do you believe in ghosts Padre?' asked a hesitant Scott.

'Ha ha, I believe what the church tells me to believe my boy!' The Padre dropped his voice, 'But I do believe in the human spirit, alive and in death. There are so many things in this world and the next that I and my church can only imagine. Yourself is a good example,'

Scott looked sharply at the Padre, suspecting that he knew about his own supernatural experiences and that his question was really about the Grey Lady. 'Me Padre?' he asked in a quivering voice.

'Well, yes. You're a fine example. You were at deaths door after your accident on the helicopter in Afghanistan. They had to place you on life support. You lost a lot of blood I believe and took several big bangs to your head. No-one knew if you would survive or how you would be when you finally came out of your coma. The brain is a complex bit of engineering that God cleverly created. But he also made it so fragile for reasons of his own. You've nursed many brain injury patients and not all come out of it well. Many have changed personalities and are no longer recognised by their loved ones as the fun or loving person they once were. Some can no longer care for themselves or do simple tasks. You were very lucky. All our prayers were answered. I know you had many months of physiotherapy, speech therapy and other treatments, but you're still you. Anyway let's not talk of the past or ghosts anymore. Tuck in my dear boy, baked beans on toast are lovely when they are hot, you must try grated cheese on top next time.'

Scott ate more of his beans on toast, feeling better already, now he knew why his patients didn't need so many painkillers after a visit from this lovely man. He was still unsure if he should say anything about his visits from the grey lady ghost, wondering where Naomi had got too and if she'd mind the Padre eating her scoff.

'So how's your health, no more fits and headaches I hope, though you are looking a bit peaky lad,' observed the Padre.

'No fits, but a stonker of a headache today, tired I think.'

'Not surprised Scott, not surprised. Good that you are back safely and back to work though,' replied the Padre clearing up his plate as he moved to the kettle. 'Let me make us a brew.' He looked puzzled again as he saw two mugs laid out by the kettle. 'So has anyone else been to see you?'

'No just you Padre.'

'Ah,' replied the Padre looking worryingly at Scott. 'Just us?'

'Aye, it's nice to get back home, away from it all. It is nice to see you again,' replied Scott as he unwrapped the chocolates. If I remember right from Afghanistan you are a toffee man?'

'That's right dear boy,' replied the Padre as he selected his favourite treat, 'nothing wrong with your memory, but plenty wrong with my teeth. And mine recalls that it is milk with no sugar for you?'

'No, nothing at all wrong with my memory, though sometimes I wish there were, it would be easier to forget some things. Yes please, milk no sugar.' Scott put the box of chocolates in front of the Padre, knowing he wouldn't be able to resist one, or even several.

'Yes, I know there were lots of things you witnessed in Afghanistan that you'd rather forget,' he replied as he eagerly selected and popped a toffee into his mouth. 'The most brutal war of our time, even in the relative safety of the hospital you saw some awful things. They were probably sights that no NHS nurse would expect to see in his or her lifetime. Yet you and your team coped admirably day in day out for months on end. And as for what happened out with the MERT, well no wonder you get nightmares my dear boy.'

'Aye, seeing poor Naomi and her squad blown up was the worst, wish my memory would stop replaying that at night,' replied Scott staring into the chocolate tray, not really taking note of the flavours and types of treats.

Padre Caldwell handed Scott his mug of tea, chewing away as he sat back down, sighing heavily whilst reaching out for another treat from the box. 'Yes your generation saw some troubling sights. It can't have been easy seeing what happened to your sweetheart. No one blames you for trying to reach her. Everyone on the enquiry was on your side. Me especially, I think I bothered my Good Lord with an abundance of prayers for you that day.'

'Aye, I ken, for what little good I did, falling over and becoming a casualty myself. I'm such a great big numptee.'

'Well not everyone can be action heroes like Naomi, she saved that lad's life, he was lucky to get onto the helicopter when he did, beside from what I hear your previous tour in Iraq saw you prove yourself, quite the action man, the nurses told me about your previous exploits when you were in intensive care. I sure am glad to see you up and about now, when you were flown back to go to Birmingham you were still on the ventilator.'

Scott rubbed his throat, where the small tracheostomy tube scar was, he didn't recall any of this, just a gradual awareness at Birmingham weeks later. Though the dreams he had were so vivid, well nightmares really. 'Naomi helped me through the worst times.'

'Yes,' replied a hesitant Padre, the worried look on his face again. 'Are the nightmares still quite bad?'

'Aye,' replied Scott, 'and I think some hallucinations.'

'Hallucinations? prompted the Padre.'

'They're much like the ones I had at Headley and Birmingham, they seem so real, like I can reach out and touch the person I'm seeing, I smell odd things as well. I can feel what's happening in the hallucinations; almost take part in these strange scenes.'

The Padre shivered as a cold draft of air swept over his body. 'Sounds like you need to tell your doctor this Scott; it doesn't sound normal to me. Perhaps it's the stress of moving in and your recent posting.'

Scott looked through to the closed bedroom door, 'aye, that's fit everyone keeps telling me.'

8

His was a brutal war, as was all wars. Hers was equally as ghastly and like Scott she was near to the frontline, especially at the Casualty Clearing Station. At times it was little more than 100 yards from the fighting, bombs exploding near to the tents, debris raining down amongst her patients. The RAMC medics did their best, bringing casualties in from their Regimental Aid Posts with bandages hastily tied on in an effort to staunch the heavy blood flow from emaciated limbs. Having to go straight back with whatever stretchers they could find, knowing that they would be immediately put to use by the brave stretcher bearers whose role was to go into the thick of it and ignore their own safety to bring back the screaming wounded.

Once, a nurse and doctor were killed outright when fragments of a bomb were hurled through the tents; piercing canvas and then seeking out flesh. Shards penetrated deep into bones from head to toe with burning metal and mud. They died instantly, their cries probably of surprise rather than pain. Each dropped down dead in front of the patients they were tending, saving their lives with their human shield. She recalled her disbelief and running over to tend to her fallen colleagues only to discover that there was nothing she

could do other than hold their dead cooling hands whilst she spoke

aloud a prayer. Then watching helplessly as the orderlies removed

their bodies and placed them in the nearby tent with the other dozens

of dead soldiers who would be buried in a mass grave the next day,

until one day, hopefully soon, when the war was over and they would

have a more respectful graveyard and individual plots. She had

attended too many ceremonies between battles for valiant soldiers,

nursing sisters, doctors and orderlies over these long months. She

constantly feared that it would be her turn one day, or that dear

Hugh would be amongst the wounded or dead. She always checked

faces before starting any treatment, sighing guiltily as she stooped

over the stretchers, ignoring her growing back pain; at ease that it

was someone else's loved one and not hers lying broken before her.

She worked twice as hard at the CCS to overcome her guilt.

She had delved deep into the psyche of Scott and knew he had

witnessed the destructive nature of man against man. He had seen

much battlefield trauma in two wars. He had coped. Though such

memories had tried to destroy his mind he was strong willed and would cope with the burden of her memories, visions that she would

now share with him. Her story would now be told.

As Scott closed the front door after saying goodbye to the Padre he heard Naomi open their bedroom door. Over his shoulder he told her that the Padre had eaten her beans on toast.

'Not to worry, I'm never hungry these days and I know how much the Padre likes his scoff.'

Scott smiled and turned to her. She was now wearing her combat uniform, boots, black beret with maroon tear dropped backing behind her Royal Army Medical Corps cap badge. *She always looks fit in her uniform* he thought. 'Are you off somewhere love?' he enquired.

'Yes. I'm taking over guard duty from Paula. She's just phoned and begged a favour. Her daughter, Alice, was taken ill at a sleepover with her friend and wants to see she's alright until her husband returns from night duty at the factory in the morning. Hope you don't mind, I really couldn't say no. Besides you look like you need a good night's sleep. I'm sorry that I missed Padre Caldwell; though I did hear his thunderous voice through the walls!'

Scott laughed, 'Aye, he disnae ken how to talk quietly does he?'

Naomi laughed with him, 'No, I wonder what he's like at funerals, though I think funerals should be a celebration of the life of what that person has achieved, not black suits and solemn faces. Promise me you'll have Padre Caldwell cracking jokes at mine one day.'

Scott reached over to his fiancée and stroked down the side of her face and round to her neck, drawing her closer to him. 'Time for a bosie you lovely lass,' he said softly as he pulled her to him, enjoying her warmth and the soft feel of her skin next to his face. 'I hope your funeral won't be for a long time yet, I want to grow old with you and have lots of adventures together.'

'You daft lump,' said Naomi, giving Scott a cheeky pat on his bum. 'Promise me you'll go straight to bed and have a good sleep. I'll be home in the morning. I'm bound to be able to catch a few hours' sleep in-between stag duties. I'll drive with you to work in the morning and have a nice run home.'

Scott spluttered, 'But that's about eight miles!'

Naomi laughed again, 'You bed pan pushers are right lazy, we medics think nothing of an eight mile run before breakfast! Anyway I'd better be off or I'll be late.' She kissed him and ruffled his hair, 'and have a shower, you are starting to smell Mr Stinky!'

Scott reached over and opened the front door with his left hand, whilst raising his right arm up and smelling his armpits, 'Mmm oxters o an Aberdeen loon, cannae beat it!' Naomi laughed as she went out into the corridor towards the communal front lobby, waving goodbye with one arm and pinching her nose with the other. She turned briefly and gave him an affectionate wink and was gone.

He gently closed the door, still sensitive to noise after his headache, which he gratefully acknowledged was gone, turned and came face to face with the smiling blue eyed face of the nursing sister.

'Jesus!' he shouted out. He took a step backwards, banging into the mirror on the wall. He turned to catch it as it wobbled. Stopping its rocking he caught a glimpse of his pale face and bedraggled hair and looked closer into the mirror. She was not there, he was hallucinating again. He breathed deeply in through his nose and let a steady breath out of his mouth. He closed his eyes and said aloud. 'You are not there.' As he steadied his breathing he opened his eyes and looked into the mirror, satisfied that he had at least controlled this hallucination, was able to put into practice what he had been taught by the psychiatric nurse at Headley Court. He closed his eyes and turned around, ready to face his fear, expecting to just see the blue flowery wallpaper that Naomi had so carefully chosen with him at The Range shop on Ivy Road in Aldershot. He pictured this fun time in his mind, like the psychiatric nurse had taught him, remembering his feelings, sights and smells, concentrating his mind away from the horrible hallucination onto something memorable and pleasant; spending time with Naomi. Only the vision was still there when he opened his eyes once more. She was beautiful. Gone was the horrifying sight of exposed bone, decaying maggot infested flesh and nerve endings. The putrefying smell of decay was replaced by the calming scent of lavender *and by god she was gorgeous* thought Scott. *If only all his hallucinations could be this pretty.* She had bowed her head, almost as if apologising for startling him. *Was she really there?* He could see hair pins where she had secured her veil. She was wearing a scarlet tippet, this cape in bright contrast to the dull grey dress that reached down below her knees, almost to her ankles where she wore thick black hosiery and old fashioned ankle boots. Much like those sisters pictured on the World War One pages of the QARANC history Facebook page he was looking at last week. Can he be imagining things again? She raised her head and looked

112

directly at him, he met her gaze and got lost in those blue eyes, feeling faint from the overpowering smell of lavender and wearing just his t-shirt and jeans he started to feel cold. It wasn't the cold of a room without heating, but a deep cold to his bones mingled with fear, piercing his soul. His head started to swim and still she locked eyes with him, entrancing him into her world, drawing him in and then his world exploded around him.

Gone was the blue flowery walls and silence of the flat but for the barking dog in the distance, biding goodnight to the neighbourhood. Instead there was a sudden explosion; earth was thrown up around him. He instinctively ducked and his hand squelched into mud. Everywhere was mud, his trainers were sucked into the wet cold earth and there was such noise. He looked up at this strange new world to see several large green canvas tents with plastic windows on the sides. Khaki clad soldiers with dirty Red Cross armbands were running around with their canvas bags banging against their sides as they carefully weaved amongst the rope lines that secured this makeshift hospital, most with stretchers carried between them. There were several wooden carts being pulled by several men. On board, tightly packed, were filthy groaning men, pink brown coloured bandages bulged with blood that continued to seep out onto the small gaps on wooden floorboards or over mud encrusted uniforms. Scott noticed that several of the men were missing arms and legs, some shorn off at the shoulder or high up at the thigh. Behind them two field ambulances motored slowly, weaving their way through the throng of people, their flickering headlights capturing the ensuing mayhem at episodic intervals. He looked up to the grey lady who reached out her hand as if to help him back onto his feet. He ignored her help, not wanting to make contact with her least she draw him further into this nightmare. 'This isn't a vison or hallucination is it?' he croaked through his suddenly dry lips. She shook her head. 'Do you mean me harm?' he pleaded. Again she shook her head. 'This is what you went through, where you nursed?' This time she slowly nodded and her eyes grew warmer to Scott, who now on his feet, simply resigned himself and said 'Show me,' and took her hand.

'Please Sister, stay away, I'm dirty, full of lice and fleas. Help the others, they need you more,' pleaded the blood and mud splattered soldier. The QA nursing sister merely calmed him down, assuring him that her freshly oiled rubber boots, taped down cuffs at her sleeves and freshly applied bandages that had been soaked in carbolic solution would help prevent being infected by the tell-tale fine white grains of sand on his tunic which revealed that he was infected with lice that not only itched but could carry the dangerous Typhus fever. Stooping down to the stretcher she helped him sit up and careful not to disturb the bloodied bandage wrapped around his head helped him to undress. Scott looked away and across the other side of the bed saw a man stretching out his arms around him, feeling around the area by his stretcher. He was shouting incoherently, yellow liquid frothing from his nose and mouth. He had read about these symptoms of a Chlorine gas attack, soon the poor blinded sod would develop acute bronchitis which would lead to pneumonia, congesting his lungs and in turn cause heart failure. There would be little the nurses and doctors could do, not even if antibiotics had been invented in this war. Soon he'd be coughing up thick green phlegm in heaving spasms between appalling bouts of breathlessness. Yellow liquid would froth from his nostrils and mouth, a sign of congestion of the lungs. He knew the doctors would try valiantly to save his life with stimulants of strychnine to try and make his heart pump better but nothing would relieve the lung congestion and heart failure, not even the salt and water emetics from the nurses who were also providing total nursing care to the helpless patient. If this effort to induce vomiting to clear the toxins failed then they would touch the back of the soldier's throat with their finger. Vomit would look frothy and yellowish. If this failed he would drown on land, probably in a few hours, in his own secretions, another victim of this new German weapon. Scott had seen photos of the lines of blinded men, eyes bandaged, walking in single file, one arm on the shoulder of the man in front, hoping that the leader would take them to safety. Within hours most would die, those unlucky to survive would never see or breath normally again. No amount of ammonium carbonate with vinum ipecacuanhae would save them. Oxygen may ease their breathing for a while, opium or even, if they could swallow at this late fatal stage, pituitary extract with brandy, would help their anxiety, but they would eventually die from heart failure. Some desperate doctors and nurses tried reviving them with the schafer's method of artificial respiration, commonly used to revive near drowned swimmers, but they usually stayed corpses.

They were just more victims of man's ability to destroy their fellow man in devious heartrending wicked ways. They would be buried outside, in mass graves, which is why so many Commonwealth War Graves can be found at the sites of former Casualty Clearing Stations.

He guessed he was in the Great War and that the grey lady had taken him back to a Casualty Clearing Station, probably from one of the Battles of Ypres. Given the confusion all round him they had not experienced such traumas before and learned from mistakes and changed procedures so it was probably the First Battle of Ypres in October 1914. It was certainly cold enough as he wrapped his arms around his body for comfort as well as warmth. He turned to find the Grey Lady once more by his side; she was nodding, as if reading his thoughts and confirming them to him. There must be over thirty wounded here, but he could only see two sisters by their scarlet bands and four staff nurses, dressed identically with the exception of not having these colourful stripes. All had replaced their beautiful capes in favour of the more practical white linen aprons. How did they cope with such trauma and still save lives? The RAMC doctor, the only one in this tent, was running between patients, prioritising his treatment, ordering various forms of care, making notes on each of the blood and mud dirtied field medical cards.

Bombs continued to drop outside, Scott, like the other nurses, seemed to accept their presence, they got on with their work whilst he stood watching, the silent observer. He looked closer at the nearest sister as she was reapplying a field dressing bandage tightly to a stumped leg. It was her, his nursing sister, his grey lady. He looked across to his companion, this ghost made flesh; again she nodded, acknowledging his growing understanding. 'You want me to see what you went through, the lives you saved, the different care of your soldiers, is that right?' Again there was the silent slow nod. 'Then keep showing me, I've seen worse than this in Basra.'

She took him through to another tented ward where staff nurses were administering the treatment for wound shock: hot alkaline drinks, warmth and rest with plenty of soothing reassurances that they were safe and that they would be operated on soon or evacuated further down the line to a Base Hospital. Those that had lost too much blood would receive a saline solution by large needle straight into the groin or armpit or by the Murphy method via a tube inserted into the rectum and absorbed by the blood stream. No need to worry about dignity when you'd seen your mates blown to pieces and bloodied limbs flying through the air. Most were just grateful to be alive and away from the battlefield, knowing they'd never be ordered fruitlessly over the top again. More lives could be saved with blood transfusions, but Scott knew from his interest in medical history that this life saving technique, still in early development, would not be used until later in the war, in 1917. Through the plastic window he could make out shadows moving in the other two tents to his right, masked figures were delving deep into chest cavities or sawing off useless bones, hoping to beat the all-pervading advance of gas gangrene. He didn't want to go into the third tent, sectioned off further to the left where he could sense rows and rows of dead bodies tightly packed on the floor, slowly sinking into the mud, duck boards too valuable and in short supply to be wasted on the dead when the living needed them. He violently shivered at the thought; he was wrong, very wrong. This was much worse than the sights he witnessed in Basra or any other field operations since and before.

They moved on again to the background noise of the booming guns, back to the first tent where a soldier was staring down in horrified fascination at his leg. 'I've been out in the bomb crater for hour's Sister,' he said nervously. 'I tried to wrap the field dressing around my own foot, but my hands were so shaky I couldn't rip the box open. I kept going to sleep, and each time I woke up I felt weaker and weaker and more muck got into my leg. I soon stopped bleeding but grew really weak. I'm glad the stretcher bearers found me eventually, brave lads. One copped it as they were carrying me back and his mate just grabbed me off the stretcher, threw me over his shoulder and quickly legged it. Christ we're both lucky to be alive. Several of the lads further down copped it from a gas attack. They were too slow pulling their masks down. We watched helplessly as they just ran around screaming before falling to the ground. They just knelt there and started scratching at their throats and pulling their tunics off, before falling down dead. Some of the poor bastards survived after that, what a horrible weapon that gas is. I can't feel anything though Sister, my leg is all numb and God but it stinks. What's that noise sister, that crackling noise?' asked the soldier as he looked down to his left leg, where his foot should have been. There were no toes. Just a stump which was now a mass of black dead tissue; the discarded bandages by the side on his stretcher were thick green yellow stained. The nurse tried to placate her weakened patient as she swabbed his mashed up ankle area with antiseptic solution, iodoform by the smell of things, but Scott looked once more at the Grey Lady who was shaking her head, unseen by the nurse and patient. *Gas gangrene*, Scott thought, *the poor bugger will either die or keep having parts of his leg taken off until the surgeons halt the mousy smelling advance of the gas bubbles that crackled beneath the touch.*

It wasn't just soldiers who were cared for by the nurses. They themselves were prone to injury, disease and illness. So much so that a special Sick Sisters Ward was set up in many General Hospitals. Chilblains were a painful condition caused by being constantly on their feet for 12 to 20 hours a day. They would find it painful to walk and had to be evacuated down the line, sometimes with the very men they had been trying to treat. Some were even evacuated by ambulance mid-shift, stricken down with fatigue or disease, some mortally wounded by nearby shelling. One staff nurse who was killed was Nelly Spindler who nursed at the 44th Casualty Clearing Station at Brandhoek. Despite heavy shelling on the 21 August 1917 her fellow QAs and RAMC doctors continued to care for patients. Sadly one shell landed on the tented hospital and wounded Nelly.

Her colleagues tried in vain to treat her abdominal wound but she died within minutes. The 44th CCS moved that day to Lijssenthoek where Nelly was buried the next day.

Special accommodation was built at Rouen, Etaples and Boulogne for the survivors for treatment from their peers and all important convalescence. There was even a villa at Hardelot set up as a convalescent home for the nursing sisters and staff nurses. Many bravely returned to frontline duties at these Casualty Clearing Stations.

Other men looked like they had developed frostbite, caused by wet trench conditions and not being able to move about. Nurses were cutting away the black and blistered skin from their toes. They then dusted down the remaining raw skin with boric, zinc oxide and amylum powder before giving a gentle massage of healthier skin and then the remaining toes were wrapped in gauze and cotton wool. These soldiers would be placed on bed rest, the bandages thought to help restore and improve circulation. They would enjoy a nutritious diet in an effort to improve healing. This included four hourly egg flips, chicken broth and brandy with milk. In some units, mostly in the home front, though some further back in France and Belgium, there were specialist masseurs available to help increase circulation with these type of wounds and many other cases.

Pain relief was basic, usually simple aspirin or for worse cases it would be morphine or potassium bromide. The advantage of the stronger two was that they induced a peaceful sleep, important after the horrors they had lived through and now amongst the bustle of the doctors, nursing sisters, staff nurses and orderlies. Other priorities after pain relief and wound management were to strip the soldiers of their uniforms and to wash them. As he looked around Scott could see several nurses washing the chests, arms, legs and faces of soldiers who stank of body odours, stale urine and blood, this ingrained with the muck of trenches and the battlefields, often over many days. Orderlies seemed to be constantly running around with steaming bowls of water or removing red or dark brown soiled bowls.

In sharp contrast to all this frantic activity there were, unbelievably, several men fast asleep in bed, still fully clothed and with an array of bandages swathing their limbs, heads and bodies. He remembered though coming in after patrols in Iraq, totally dead-beat after having to stay fully alert and looking for enemy activity. The weight of his rifle, personal kit and medical gear left him shattered, the heat hadn't helped. He recalled that once at base and his kit and rifle had been cleaned he had slept for hours, only awakening for food, drinks and toilet needs. Then he went straight back to bed and deep rejuvenating sleep. It must have been ten times worse for these soldiers who had endured hours of pre-battle nerves followed by intense fighting. They had earned their sleep.

Scott empathised with them and looked away and was shocked to see the casualty across from him and in the far corner of the tent sitting upright, propped up and grinning away like a silent, but ominous ventriloquist's dummy. He looked to the grey lady who just looked back, waiting for Scott to make the connection between the muscle spasms of the neck and back which arched him more upright whilst pulling his mouth up into a rictus grin at the other patients and nurses. At his next painful spasm he groaned out loud and then Scott knew what this macabre dance like movement was. It was lockjaw; the soldier was battling tetanus from the bloody, muddy, filthy, rat infested battlefield. The grey lady nodded and delved deeper into Scott's mind, helping him to recall the treatment; peace and quiet – something he wouldn't get in this CSS so near the front – and frequent feeding of a mushed up diet to help replace lost calories due to the severe physical strain on the body caused by the involuntary spasms of this anaerobic infection. 'I think I'm seen enough now,' whispered Scott tiredly. 'Please take me back home, back to my flat and Naomi. I don't know what you want from me but please, the CMH is gone and you should find peace and go to the afterlife, Christ but after what you've been through in the war you deserve it.' Scott once more felt the deep chill and was overcome by the smell of lavender.

9

Happier memories, she sought and craved happier memories. She yearned for a time when she was happy. For a time when there was no war, just peace and time to spend with her beloved Hugh. She smiled as she remembered her two weeks leave from the venereal disease ward at the Connaught Hospital at Marlborough Lines in Aldershot, over a century ago, in 1912. Her smile widened and her eyes shone as she remembered travelling back home on the long train rides to be with Hugh. He loved to see her in her walking out uniform of the QAIMNS, her long grey dress with scarlet cuffs was so beautiful. Though the tight scarlet collar was uncomfortable, it did help correct the posture. They all sat up straight in those days, not slouched like so many of the modern women she saw before her Kingdom closed down. It was the hat that she truly missed. It was a boater style hat with scarlet, grey and white ribbon tied neatly at the front in a bow. It was so beautiful. It had cost a small fortune at Shoolbreds in Tottenham Court Road on a rare trip out to London, but worth every penny each time Hugh saw her, took a sharp breath and called her a bonnie quine. How she missed him calling her his beautiful girl. How she would blush despite her parasol protecting her from the heat of the summer sun. She was grateful for the gift of the price of her uniform from her father, knowing that she would not be able to afford it on her nurse's wage he had cabled a telegram to the tailor to request that he be invoiced. She missed her father's generosity in terms of love and not just finance and knew he had been proud of her service.

She knew what she must do. She must take Scott back to 1912, to see her in her walking out uniform, but more importantly, to see Hugh when he was handsome and whole, she would share her beloved as Scott must share his.

Scott woke to the sound of bird song, children playing and the gentle flow of water. He could smell grass and flower blossom and as his senses awakened he could now hear the gentle movement of leaves rustling on the trees. As he became more fully awake he could hear the rhythmic sweeping of paddles on water interspersed with the sound of laughter. His sight was becoming more focused and he could now see couples dressed in suits and formal dresses on small boats, the gentlemen paddling steadily with their feet. The women were sitting back and relaxing, many looking across to the island where ducks enjoyed sanctuary. He shook his head in an effort to clear his mind of this peaceful scene so soon after the carnage of World War One. 'Nah, it cannae be?' He opened his eyes once more expecting to see fresh horror. They settled on the gentle blue eyes of the Grey Lady who now wore a peaceful smile and what seemed like a twinkle in her eyes. 'So you are real aren't you?' Again there was the calm nod in acknowledgement. She widened her arms and slowly moved them around the view, sweeping them gently around allowing Scott time to follow their slow arc and take in his new surroundings. He spotted the ornate Victorian bandstand, the centre piece of the lush green grass on which children played an assortment of games with hoops and small balls. To his left he viewed the large glassed winter gardens with its high dome. He marvelled at its beauty with a hint of sadness as it shone as the summer sun reflected off the glass because he knew that one day this proud building would succumb to nature and fall in high winds. He didn't need to be told that this was the original David Welch Winter Gardens. To confirm this he looked beyond and spied the marble Temperance Fountain, so new and shiny that it even had the original metal mugs hanging from it so that day trippers could enjoy a refreshing sip of water. This clean source of liquid was made readily available to help keep the public away from the temptations of alcohol. Now he knew for sure where he was but for confirmation he turned to his right to take in the natural beauty of the River Dee, flowing gently on its way to the harbour about a mile away. As he continued his panoramic view he took in the newness of the footbridge over the boating pond. He remembered reading about this in the Press and Journal newspaper one day. It had been salvaged from the Denburn valley and explained why it looked so much like a bridge going over a railway line. The granite stone was so shiny in the sun and seemed to proudly sparkle alongside the iron supports.

'Ye hiv ta'en me hame, but fit wye?' questioned Scott who automatically started to speak in the Doric dialect of his home town. He corrected himself so that this ghost would understand him, but as he asked 'You have taken me home, but why?' he noticed that she was already nodding. She had understood his broad dialect. 'I ken that this is the Duthie Park in Aberdeen, but why here?' He turned full circle and looked across to the other side of the road towards Allenvale Cemetery that poked out over the low walls and through the small trees, not having yet reached their full potential. Scott turned to the Grey Lady with sadness in his eyes, 'Mither wouldnae be buried there for many years lass, please tell me why I'm here.' Scott lowered his head as he thought of his mother and her funeral in a much more crowded graveyard many years in this future, but only a few in his own past. He hopefully thought that perhaps this phantom had taken him to a time when his mother was still alive, but he could see her empathically shaking her head. He looked up again and saw there were few headstones, most in the plot looking over the banks of the River Dee. Looking further he spotted the familiar sight of the salmon fisherman's bothy. He turned back to the Grey Lady and saw that she was pointing to a couple walking hand in hand towards the tall granite obelisk that Scott knew commemorated Sir

James McGrigor. He had taken an interest in this on his leave visits

because it was built in memory of a surgeon in the Army Medical

Service who was famed for his many achievements, the most noted

was for improving sanitary conditions for soldiers and thus saving

many lives from potential diseases. Though it once proudly sat in the

courtyard of Marischal College, the University of Aberdeen, where

Sir James had studied and would became a Rector; it had been

moved here in 1906. Scott turned to the Grey Lady, who reading his

thoughts again nodded to confirm that they were indeed in the

Duthie Park in Aberdeen after 1906 but before the Great War. Scott

had often been inspired that a local loon had risen to the position of

Director-General of the Army Medical Department and held this

post for 36 years. He knew if a local lad could do this then he could

perhaps have a career in the Queen Alexandra's Royal Army Nursing

Corps and maybe rise in its ranks. As he thought all this he had been

unaware that he and the Grey Lady had moved to the flower bed in

front of the obelisk and would now see and hear the couple. He

looked at the now familiar face next to him, a hill of roses in bloom in the background, and then to the couple and back to the Grey Lady who was nodding at his growing understanding. 'It's you!'

'Ah've missed you lass, an our walks in our bonnie park' said the man in the brown suit, 'working on the fairm takes ma mind aff ye, but I miss you.'

'Och Hugh, you ken fine well that I feel the same way, but I love my job too. You have your father's farm to run now and I have my vocation. If Matron knew that we were engaged I'd be forced to leave nursing and the army. I feel torn between you both. Take comfort that I come home on my holidays and we can be thegither. Let's ging doon tae the boating pond an watch the men sail their model boaties.' The couple walked down the path to the long and wide but shallow boat pond where a group of men, dressed in shabbier suits and flat caps were sailing their model yachts with their children who were dressed in long socks, shorts and sleeveless pullovers. The couple stopped and gave each other a quick kiss, the lady taking her fiancé's face gently in her hands and stopping to look him long in the eyes. 'I love you Hugh and promise we will marry one day, I just want to have a few years of a career before I become a farmer's wife. I want to see a bit of the world before we settle in Cruden Bay.'

Hugh snorted, 'Aye, well, Aldershot's nae that much different fae Aiberdeen.'

'Maybe no Hugh, but some of the aulder Sisters did nurse the men in the second Boer War and often did spik aboot places like Natal, Kroonstad, Pietermaritzburg and Wynburg. And since the War Office acknowledged the important work of these Army Nursing Service Sisters and officially formed the Queen Alexandra's Imperial Military Nursing Service I want to be a part of it, even if just for a few years.' Taking his hand she continued. 'Besides you men never sit in peace, one day there will be other wars and I'd like to sit our children on my knee and tell my stories by a warm fire, just like your dear auld faither did. Please dinnae begrudge me that.'

'Och no quine,' replied Hugh with an impatient sigh, 'but it should be a man that tells war stories, nae a stotter o a lass like you. Quick, naebodies looking, gies a bosie!'

'Oh Hugh you are naughty, you know I don't like to cuddle in public, people stare so disapprovingly.'

'Well let them, they should see fit the ram gets up tae when I let him in the field wi the sheep!'

She laughed, slapped him playfully on the arm and turned back to watch the boats gently sail in the wind to the delight of their owners, Scott and the Grey Lady their silent and unseen observers.

Scott turned to the Grey Lady, 'Did you marry?'

She looked down to her black ankle shoes and shook her head sadly.

'Just who are you? Hugh didn't even mention you're name. I cannae keep ca'ing you The Grey Lady! I had a brief thought that you are Lady Elizabeth Crombie Duthie and have taken me back to see your park, but she gifted it to the City in 1880 when she was an auld wifie an you are young. She died a few years later without ever having had children, so you are not her daughter. I ken you can understand the Doric and you speak with a local accent, you're a fellow Aberdonian aren't you?' She nodded, continuing her silence. 'Aye, well richt enough, the CMH has been closed for years an I bet you've forgotten how tae spik, or did something shocking happen tae make you dumb?'

Not liking this, the Grey Lady snarled at Scott, once more turning to bone and teeth before him, saliva spraying onto his face during the sudden transformation. Scott took a step back, overcoming his fear he said apologetically, 'Sorry lass, but this is all affa strange tae me. One minute I'm enjoying being back at work and the next I'm transported tae a Casualty Clearing Station in France during a fierce bombardment and then whipped home to see my favourite park next to where my mum's going to be buried. I'm sure this is all another hallucination, but if it's nae then please just take me hame to Naomi and leave me alone.'

She softened again, the grimace slowly disappearing from her skull as flesh once more formed and was replaced with the peaceful features of a pale skinned Nursing Sister in scarlet and grey uniform. This time she reached out her hand to take Scott's and as he felt the cold softness of her small hand he was once more overcome with the heady smell of lavender, 'Scott, Scott, can you hear me' he heard as he drifted off...

'Scott, Scott, can you hear me Scott?' shouted a worried Naomi. She sat on the edge of the bed, still wearing her combats from last night. Scott was collapsed on the bed, feverish and burning up. He quickly opened his startled eyes which softened when he saw who it was shouting his name and pawing at his shoulder.

'Alright love, you can stop hammering on my shoulder now!' He gave himself a rub as if to soothe his shoulder, 'Guard duty over with already?'

'It's eight in the morning Scott.' He sat upright and reached for his iPhone on the bedside cabinet.

'It can't be I only went to bed a few minutes ago.'

Naomi put her hand over his forehead, 'I thought you were having an early night. You look even worse this morning and I think you've got a temperature. You feel really hot.'

'Aye. Well, I've had an eventful night love.'

'Oh?' enquired a puzzled Naomi.

'Aye, but I dinnae think you'll believe me,' replied a worried Scott.

'Try me.'

'Ballocks!' shouted Scott as he jumped up from the bed after seeing the time on the screen. 'It really is after eight. Brilliant, that's just brilliant. Second day on the job and I'm late. I should have been on shift thirty minutes ago. Look, could you please phone Major Dunn and say I was ill through the night and make my apologies?' Scott tried to hand her the phone.

Naomi ignored it, 'No Scott, I think it would be better coming from you, I'll make you a coffee.' Naomi turned smartish and left the bedroom while Scott searched for Major Dunn's number and pressed to call it.

After several rings he heard 'Major Dunn speaking.'

'Hello Sir,' replied an apologetic sounding Scott, 'sorry about this but it's Corporal Grey here, I'm afraid I've slept in, I didn't have a good night last night.'

There was a brief silence on the other end followed by a sighed 'What happened and how are you now Grey?'

'I think I had hallucinations or bad dreams Sir, I just remember going to bed and being woken up this morning feeling rough. I don't think I could manage a shift Sir.'

'I see Grey, though I'm not surprised, I did think getting you back to work full time so soon was the wrong decision. I wanted you to take some leave then ease back into things but against my advice you opted for fulltime. Look, take the day off but report to your doctor as soon as you can and phone me at nine in the morning tomorrow with an update. You've been through a lot and we're all on your side, we just want to see you back to your normal self. Don't even think about driving today, just rest.'

'Thank you Sir,' replied Scott and hung up as Naomi came back into the room. 'I've got the day off, I think I'll go back to sleep. Did you make a coffee?'

'Oh no, I forgot,' said a sheepish Naomi. 'But come through to the kitchen and make one for yourself and tell me about last night, did you have bad dreams again?'

Scott walked through with her to the kitchen. 'I think so, though they were so vivid. I think I've been reading too many books on the history of military nursing, I might put them away for a few weeks.'

'Oh, why's that?' asked Naomi.

'Well I had dreams, though they were more hallucinations. One minute I'm standing in the hallway after saying goodbye to you, and then I turn around and I'm staring straight into an old fashioned dressed Nursing Sister.'

Naomi laughed, 'I'm glad she was dressed. Should I be worried that you have a thing for older nurses in uniform?'

'No, be serious, I think I'm going crazy or being haunted.'

'Haunted?' asked a worried Naomi.

'Aye, she was dressed like the skeleton I told you about earlier; only she had a beautiful face and looked like flesh and blood, like a real person. She transported me back into her past to a CCS in France.'

'What, during World War One?' asked Naomi whilst pointing to a pile of history books on the kitchen windowsill.

'Aye, well, I'll not be reading those for a while. They are making me dream odd things, though it was so real, as if I really was there. Then she whisked me to Aberdeen.'

'Ha ha, quicker than the sleeper train then,' joked Naomi. 'If only we could drive back to see your dad so quickly.'

'No, be serious love, I really felt like I was there. Only it wasn't this century, it was the last I think judging by the way everyone was dressed.'

'Sounds fine, did you have a couple of butteries from the bakery,' replied a sarcastic Naomi referring to the Aberdeen breakfast delicacy of a lard laden flat morning roll which tasted like a dense salty croissant which she knew Scott really loved and missed.

'I wish! She took me to the Duthie Park, just before World War One, I even saw mum's graveyard, only where she was buried was still grassed, just the front area had headstones. '

'Er, okay, why would a ghostie, your new mistress, take you back home, not buy you breakfast and instead show you around a park,' joked Naomi still in sarcasm mode.

'She wanted to show me how happy she was before the war with her fiancé, his name was Hugh, a well-built handsome chap who was a farmer,' replied Scott earnestly.

'Ah, caught you out, you've always told me that early QAs had to devote themselves to the job and had to leave nursing if they got married. Mmm, tell me more about handsome Hugh though!' joked Naomi.

'Aye, I did,' confirmed Scott ignoring her request, 'but they kept their relationship secret, only seeing each other during leave in Aberdeen. I think she lived there because he had a farm in Cruden Bay.'

Naomi smiled, remembering a pleasant forty minute drive from Aberdeen, followed by a lovely walk along golden sands there by the sea, a quick visit to a ruined Castle that Scott had tried to convince her was the inspiration for Bram Stoker to write Dracula, followed by a tasty lunch in the St Olaf Hotel restaurant. Scott's eyes proved bigger than his belly when he was defeated by their huge mixed grill, unable to finish the moist black pudding. Scott was animated about the old black and white photographs in the dining room of the surrounding area like the Bullars of Buchan rock formation by the sea. This beautiful attraction was a collapsed sea cave with a natural arch running over the circular chasm and was a haven for birdlife, including some adorable puffins. They visited it after their lunch to burn off their excess calories. But not before Scott had seen the old Cruden Bay Hotel photo and gave her what seemed a half hour lecture about how it used to be the 1st No1 Scottish General Hospital for the Territorial Force during World War Two and had been requisitioned by the War Office in 1938. She learned over lunch that after their training these volunteer nurses and doctors, recruited locally and from the TA unit at Aberdeen Royal Infirmary, then embarked to Egypt to form the 15th Scottish General Hospital. Naomi had hoped Scott would take her for afternoon tea at this old Hotel on a return visit but was disappointed to learn that it had been demolished and now formed part of the golf course. 'So you dreamed all this last night while I was on duty, no wonder you're so tired and ill.'

Scott reached out and took her hand. 'I felt her do this to me, when she brought me home. She was so cold, like a corpse, but looked so real, so alive. I ken you think I've gone crazy again, but I haven't. I'm being haunted by the Grey Lady, in this very building that used to be the Cambridge Military Hospital. Come on, you've heard the stories, how she would come out and sit by the dying or help the dead cross over to the other side. Do you think she's come for me, has my head injury done something to me?'

Naomi turned pale 'Please Scott, you're beginning to scare me. You know I believe in ghosts, but I don't want to see one, let alone have one take my husband to be away from me. Please tell me you just had bad dreams or aren't ready to go back to work and are joking with me. You know I scare easy. Dead and mangled bodies I can cope with, give me blood and guts, but not ghosts. Don't you remember when you took me to Edinburgh Dungeons and that actor dressed as an executioner jumped out at me in the dark and I screamed my head off and nearly pissed myself.'

Chuckling away at the memory Scott replied, Aye, nearly wet yourself, your language is getting bad love; those Jocks had a bad influence.'

Looking sad at the memory of her fallen comrades Naomi frowned and said quietly, 'Bless them, but my language would be a lot worse if I came face to face with a ghostie. Anyway I think you'd better get yourself something to eat and drink, you'll feel better for it, and then back to bed with you Mr Nursey.'

'Okay,' replied Scott as he filled up the kettle.

'So if his name was Hugh, what was hers?' asked Naomi.

'That's the odd thing, she never speaks to me, and when her past self was talking to Hugh, he used pet names for her, but never spoke her name.'

Naomi laughed once more, 'It really is sounding like a male fantasy, a nurse in uniform who doesn't talk and so won't answer you back! If she's taking you on these dates you really should find out her name Scott!'

'I think I know it Naomi, I think I know what she wants from me. It can't be a coincidence that the medals I've collected all belong to the same Nursing Sister or that I've seen her trying to open the cabinet and that they fell off the wall. I think they belonged to her and now

she wants them back, or she wants me for some other reason.'

10

He was getting closer to learning her story now, but more must be told. She wanted him to learn about poor dear Hugh and what he went through at the Battle of Loos on the 15 September 1915. She was so proud when he enlisted into the army on the day war broke out. He travelled from the farm at Cruden Bay to the recruiting office in Aberdeen, impatient and not wanting to wait for the Regimental Recruiting Sergeant who came to the local village weeks later. Hugh had looked magnificent in his black and green with yellow over stripe kilted uniform with khaki battledress jacket. The yellow sat centre to the kilt and if he had been an officer he would have proudly worn a kilt with two yellow stripes. Hugh was one of the lucky ones to be issued with the full and correct kit. Many recruits, especially in the early eager rush to enlist, were issued khaki kilts due to shortages. He stood straighter too and walked taller in his brogues, even the red and black diced hose tops seemed to make him grow an extra inch. She loved the cocky way that he wore his Glengarry on the top of his head at a slight angle with his white gunmetal Gordon Highlanders badge of the stag head surrounded by a wreath of ivy to each side. "By Dand" was proudly stated underneath the cap badge: steadfast was this motto's meaning and she knew and later learned of the fierce and loyal way that each member of this magnificent Regiment fought. The words were taken from her native Doric dialect from the words Byde and Fecht which meant stay and fight. Over the centuries that the Regiment existed, it was eventually abbreviated to the first two words and reshaped.

In those early days Hugh was ready to take on the Germans, despite only recently passing swiftly through the Regimental Depot of the Gordon Highlanders at Castlehill Barracks. He still had to complete his basic training at the King Street Militia Barracks where the 3rd (Reserve) Battalion, the new service battalions, took responsibility for the training of the 8th Battalion to which Hugh now belonged. Over 800 officers and 20,000 men would pass through here and be trained for Front Line duties.

By the time she next had a letter from him he was stationed at Aldershot as part of the First New Army and the 26th Brigade of the 9th (Scottish) Infantry Division. He was completing his advanced training before movement to France. From his writings he sounded *much more confident and from the enclosed photograph he was*

much broader built and looked ready for action.

He later moved to Bordon and drew nearer to her when he was

mobilised to Boulogne and straight into the thick of the Western

Front. She was already there, nursing the wounded at Number 2

Casualty Clearing Station at Bailleul and already searching

wounded faces hoping that none were her beloved Hugh. But she

was saved the grief of seeing him wounded and in great pain, almost

dying, before her colleagues at No.20 Casualty Clearing Station at

St Omer performed life-saving surgery in the converted boarding

school that cost him his leg from the bullet wound and gas gangrene,

but it meant she would see him once more. If only they did not have

to keep their love a secret because of her position. She was glad

though that her nerves had gotten the better of her and that her

Matron in Chief, Miss Ethel Hope Becher, had fortuitously posted

her to the CMH in Aldershot where her beloved Hugh was

recuperating. This esteemed Matron in Chief not knowing one of her

top Nursing Sisters was not battle shocked from nursing so near the

front line for two years, but was distraught at not seeing her

wounded fiancée and was beside herself at not being able to be with him because Nursing Sisters were not expected to be engaged to be married and keep on nursing. She could only learn how he was from his occasional letters to her, or from his parents, which is how she had first learned of his injuries. It had been too much for her to cope with emotionally, though she tried at Hugh's insistence that she was needed to care for more like him. He was always thinking of others, a quality she greatly admired in him. Sometimes, in her darkest days, her guilt at what she considered her selfishness ate away at her. Though of course how anyone could be expected to keep nursing the wounded and dying when their own loved one needed them more. Now was the time to show Scott Hugh's story, if only Naomi would leave his side like she had reluctantly had to leave Hugh's.

'Now you really are scaring me Scott,' said a nervous Naomi. 'You can't mean that you'll be haunted by the Grey Lady until you give her back her medals? How on earth do you give a ghost back her belongings?' She shivered as she asked this question, noticing that the room was getting colder. 'What possible reason would she want you for? Do you think this room was her old ward, or maybe even where she died?' She quivered as she looked around. 'And why is it only you who sees her? Not that I want to see her, this is all giving me the creeps. Don't you think it's time you went to see your doctor?'

Ignoring her concerns for his mental health Scott continued with his thoughts aloud to Naomi. 'It's almost as if she's telling me about herself. I suspect who she is. But I don't know much about her, though I could find out more about her online at National Archives or at the Army Medical Services Museum at Keogh, but they'd think I was mad investigating a ghost. Can you imagine! They'd be keeping me blethering whilst the Curator phoned for the men in white coats! I'd be discharged from the army quicker than a Para up an assault course wall. I suspect she died without family, so I can't say I'm researching my family history. Though I suppose I could tell the researchers that I have an interest because she is a fellow Aberdonian and fellow QA. She's showed me so much about her life but yet can't share her name.'

Scott walked through to the spare room where his desk and laptop was. He switched on the power and turned to chat to Naomi who had entered the room, she had her arms wrapped about her. 'Are you cauld love?'

'Yes, both rooms have been getting colder.' She shivered as Scott stooped down and felt the radiator.

'The heating seems to be working fine.'

'I hope I'm not going down with whatever bug you may have, though I think you just need to rest and stop this nonsense.'

'It's not nonsense,' retorted Scott beginning to get fed up that she wouldn't believe him. 'So many QAs and patients from the old Cambridge Military Hospital have reported strange sightings and occurrences over the years. It has to be true, with so many similar stories. She's real, she's here and she wants me for something.'

Naomi put her arms around Scott to reassure him, 'I want you for something!'

Scott, enjoying the embrace, cuddled her tightly back. He then reluctantly removed himself from the hug and smiled at her lovingly.

'Maybe later!' he laughed, regretting his brief outburst. 'But I have to do this; I have to find out what she wants. I really feel that she is reaching out for me and needing my help.' He sat down by the laptop and clicked on the internet and began searching for the National Archives. When he got there he chose the *search our records* section and got through to their online collection. He then clicked on *find a person* and shouted in delight 'Look!' He pointed to the screen and showed Naomi the section for find a British army nurse under the Army Personnel section. 'I didn't think it would be so easy.'

Naomi sat on the spare chair, her curiosity aroused. 'Gosh, I didn't realise you could search so easily, look at all the choices. You could practically find out about anyone from years ago. I wonder what it will say about me when I'm long dead?'

Scott turned to her and patted her hands, 'Let's hope that's not for a long time yet sweetie.'

Naomi pointed to the screen. 'Come on, I'm dying to find out who this other woman in your life is.'

Scott clicked on the British Army Nurses link and started to read the new page. 'Wow, you can access the service records of nurses who served with the army during the Great War. She was definitely a World War One nurse from the visions she showed me.' Scott clicked this new link for WO399. 'That should take me to the relevant War Office documents.' Reading the screen he was surprised to read that there was over 15,000 First World War service records for nurses, though these also included the Reserve and the Territorial Force Nursing Service. Scott knew he could omit the TFNS from his search since their role was to serve around Great Britain in the 23 Territorial Hospitals which were controlled by the War Office and under Army administration. He knew the Grey Lady was definitely a QAIMNS Nursing Sister from her uniform and because she had served at the Frontline. He could search by first and surname. 'Ah, I have to pay to read them online or visit them at Kew to see them in person for free. I don't fancy a drive to Richmond, especially as I've phoned in sick. I can't be seen going all the way to Surrey instead of working. I'll just get my wallet from the bedroom and pay by credit card to see her files now.' Scott rose to his feet and turning he saw a worried looking Naomi.

'I'm really cold Scott, my feet are so numb, could you please check the heating is switched on?'

'Sure. But it feels really warm, I shan't be a minute.' He made his way to the kitchen where he checked the heating controls. 'Everything looks fine love,' he shouted through to Naomi, 'and it's lovely and toasty warm here. I'll check the bedroom heater and grab my wallet.' As he made his way down to the bedroom he heard a blood curdling scream come from Naomi and the spare room door slammed shut with an almighty crash. Scott ran to it and tried to push it open, but it was shut stiff. No amount of pushing was going to shift it. 'Naomi!' he frantically shouted, 'are you alright, what's happening, I cannae get in.'

When Scott had left the room, Naomi reached down to her feet to rub them to get them warm. When she had removed her boots and socks she was shocked to see her feet were pitted and blue and that no amount of rubbing would warm them up or return the circulation to them. As she was rubbing furiously to get some heat to them she noticed that her hands were similarly blue and also numb. This feeling was throughout her whole body and the coldness could not be shaken off. She stood up to go to Scott and as she turned she caught a whiff of lavender and there in front of her was the Grey Lady, smiling and reaching out for her hand.

Naomi backed away, not in fright of this spectre but in fear of what would happen next. She looked a lovely nursing sister, not as a grotesque skeleton like Scott had described but as a beautiful young woman, in the prime of her life, full of radiance and with enthusiastic eyes that beamed kindly down at Naomi, almost motherly despite her youthful appearance. Naomi was drawn to her, despite a gnawing fear itching to get out and overcome her. The Grey Lady's old fashioned uniform was immaculately ironed and crisp, so clean, the white veil radiant in sharp contrast to the bright scarlet of her tippet. Her right hand was stretching out for Naomi who started to back away, her fear now overcoming any sense of awe at this vision. Naomi sensed that despite the beautiful appearance of this ghost that it wanted her for some terrible purpose, to take her away from Scott. 'Fuck off, you are not real,' shouted Naomi, gathering her courage, and remembering her battlefield training with the Jocks took the battle to the enemy and advanced to this spectre. 'Maybe Scott's daft enough to believe in you and go on travels with you but I am not. Now do one or you'll get my size sixes up you!'

The Grey Lady snarled at this advancing impertinent woman, her beauty briefly transformed into frightening bone and bared teeth that leaned forward to Naomi in a menacing ruffle of uniform, her tippet, veil and dress rising above her to shroud over her diminutive figure.

'Just fuck right off and leave us both alone you bitch, go back to hell or whichever nightmare you came from. Your theatricals don't scare me, just get to fuck,' screamed Naomi as she gathered her courage and aimed her fist at this vision to try and knock it out of the way.

The skeleton swayed back, its head appearing to distance itself casually from the neck, its vertebrae pulling itself backwards and twisting at the pelvis. As it moved to the left its right claws, finger bones with unnaturally long nails attached to them, moved back to Naomi, this time its index finger pointing at her, appearing to waggle as if in disgust at the foul language or telling Naomi off for trying to strike her.

Naomi mistook this macabre finger bone dance as mocking her and in outrage tried to knock the jiggling bones apart. She watched in disbelief at the way this skeleton could remain intact without ligaments, tendons and muscles to hold them together and help movement. She could not believe the speedy way that this fleshless carcasses frame was moving to avoid her punches. *If this is truly what Scott has been seeing then no wonder he's going mad again,* she thought as she tried to figure out what to do next. 'Alright bitch, move aside so I can let Scott in or I'll tear you bone from bone, you've picked the wrong girl to mess with.' With that, Naomi leapt directly at the grey dress, hoping to rugby tackle the vision to the ground. The Grey Lady moved swiftly aside, bones jangling against each other in mock musical tribute to Naomi's performance. They reformed themselves inside the uniform, the skull clicking last into place as the veil slide smoothly over to sit perfectly once more to complete the perfect uniform as veins, capillaries, muscle, and fat and then skin moulded themselves around bones to form this stunning vision. Naomi, now in an undignified pile on the floor, looked up, aghast at this gruesome sight reshaping itself. In sharp contrast the nursing sister was now standing over her, deep blue eyed and mousy haired with a serene expression of forgiveness on her face. Her hands were clasped non-threateningly at her front, as if in silent prayer. She awaited Naomi's next move.

Naomi also awaited the next move, wondering what on earth was going on. *I've just been bested by a bloody ghost!* She sat up, a look of resignation coming over her face. 'Okay, okay, I know I'm not mad, so I guess you are real and Scott's not mad either, but what the fuck do you want? Please just go and leave us alone. I just want to be with Scott.'

At this the Grey Lady shook her head slowly, with a look of sadness enveloping her eyes and spreading to her kindly mouth. She reached out her hand and Naomi felt its enticing attraction, knowing that the right thing to do was to reach out and accept the ghostly embrace. But she looked down at her uniform, remembering that she was a soldier as well as a medic, proud of the motto of her Corps, In Arduis Fidelis. It meant faithful in adversity and she thought grimly that it didn't get much more adverse than this. She snatched her hand violently away and glared at the Grey Lady 'FUCK, RIGHT, OFF, BITCH!' The Grey Lady simply looked down at Naomi, smiled, put her index finger to her pursed lips, turned and appeared to glide to the shut door and vanished. Naomi screamed 'Scott!'

Scott, hearing the screams, was trying frantically to open the door. He stepped back as far as the hallway wall, preparing to launch his shoulder against the door. As he shouted, 'Stand back Naomi, I'm going to try and burst through,' he was aware of a high pitched rushing sound as greyness enveloped him and shook him off his feet. Instead of falling over he became dizzy with the heady scent of lavender and once more felt a chilling presence. Air rushed past his ears, his hair tickling his scalp as his eyes took in the changing landscape around him. Gone was the nicely decorated hallway, instead he had brief glimpses of bricks, roads, ocean and fields rapidly passing in this maelstrom. Within seconds he sensed himself and the grey shape come to a halt and as his light-headedness receded his eyes focused on the Grey Lady, her serious looking eyes locked onto his. As he caught his breath at this sudden forced expulsion his immediate words were, 'Naomi, is Naomi alright?'

The Grey Lady nodded as she held onto Scott to stop him falling as his resolving dizziness caused him to sway.

Feeling her coldness Scott continued to ask questions in an attempt to focus his mind on what just happened. 'I heard her screaming, and then shouting, did you harm her?'

The Grey Lady kept her cold embrace on Scott and shook her head, kindly looking back.

'But she saw you, right, she now believes me.'

Again the understanding nod.

Scott sighed in relief. He was about to ask her more questions, but then he heard a high pitched whistling sound, followed by a loud thud and then an explosion shook the ground. Earth was lifted up and thrown in their direction. As his senses started to tune into his surroundings, rather than the eyes of the Grey Lady, he looked around in disbelief. He stood in a boggy deeply rutted field with areas of smoke. As the smoke eased off in sections he could make out barbed wire strewn haphazardly on the ground and also attached to wooden posts. In the distance he thought he could make out bodies lying forlorn in the mud, what limbs were left were disjointed, exposed flesh had turned putrid blue and black, rifles discarded nearby, uniforms ragged and canvas webbing belts and leather looking pouches tattered. He thought he saw a spike on one cracked black leather helmet, half buried at the back into the mud. The owners head had been stripped bare of all flesh and eyes. His hair hung loose atop the skull which still tried vainly to wear proudly the brass eagle plate of this enemy Pickelhaube head protection. Though the spike and ineffective leather material would be withdrawn and replaced with the steel made Stahlhelm, it was evidently too late for this wretched soul half buried in no man's land and left to rot. The heavily earth-caked cloth helmet cover hung limply on the side, no longer providing any form of reflective shielding against enemy light and gunfire. One severed limb still wore high black boots, caked in mud, flesh and nerves, long bled out, dangling from the top of the discoloured flesh, small teeth marks were evidence that opportunistic rats had taken this chance for an easy meal. A solitary crow swooped down from a lone branchless tree, the tall burned stump, shot with bullet holes, acting like a grisly signpost to this desolate landscape. The bird started to peck at the decayed flesh until it flew high into the air, its prize forgotten, learning not to return for this convenient snack, as another shell whistled past and exploded to decimate more barbed wire. The bird flew off, alone in the sky except for clouds of smoke dissolving slowly as more joined the floating display in the semi-darkness as dusk finally left this barren land, leaving it in pitch darkness.

'Shit!' shouted Scott. 'You've taken me to no man's land. Am I safe? Will the bombs hurt me?' he asked frantically as the earth continued to shake and the air vibrate.

The Grey Lady slowly shook her head, her calm movements hypnotising Scott as he felt his sudden panic give way to an oddly timed serenity. He took a deep breath. 'Okay, sorry, I dinnae normally swear, but these arenae normal times.' Scott thought for a second or two, trying to make order out of the chaos around him and the deep craters caused by the shelling, most filled with stagnant water from rain water that had been pouring for days. He marvelled at how the Grey Lady's uniform always looked pristine as if just freshly laundered and ironed. 'So if we are back in World War One and nurses like yourself didn't go to the trenches and certainly not into no man's land,' Scott quickly pointed to the rotting corpses, 'I'm guessing the British lines are back this way,' he continued as he turned back round. Just then a star shell burst above him and released an explosion of magnesium which lit its surroundings in a dazzling display of red and green lights like an inappropriately timed sinister firework. A small parachute fluttered open to slow its descent and provide longer light as it made its way gradually to the ground. Scott dropped to the floor, expecting enemy fire to burst around him. As he sunk into the mud he quickly placed his hands around his head in a defensive position. Nothing around him moved, there were no working parties from either side repairing the barbed wire under the cover of darkness. Nor was there anyone in the nearby observation slit trench listening out for any enemy movement, ever alert to anyone taking advantage of the dark between star shells to repair defences or mount an attack, trying hard not to move in case an enemy shooter took them out during this dangerous listening role. There were not even working parties tasked to repair or replace the traverses, the safety buttresses that supported the trenches at equally spaced out intervals. No soldier was filling sandbags with earth as ballast against shots and shells. No man's land was still, the star shell fell uselessly to the floor, spent and provided no guiding light for a deadly sniper's bullet. The chemical reaction burned itself out and fizzled to nothingness as the small cloth parachute landed nearby. All the soldiers were resting and preparing themselves for the forthcoming battle. Their leaders were confident that they would gain land and no longer need these trenches, they would soon command the German trenches. Scott rose from the ground, brushed himself down, surprised that there was no mud on his clothes.

All the time the Grey Lady remained standing, waiting patiently for Scott. There was another nod of the head to convey she had understood his earlier question, she pointed her narrow hand to where Scott was now looking and with the other she was beckoning him.

'No, wait a minute, I want some answers first of all,' demanded Scott, realising he was safe from enemy fire because he was unable to interact with his surroundings and that others in this nightmare were unable to see or harm him. He was a silent observer. 'First I want your promise that you'll take me back to Naomi and that she's unharmed.'

The Grey Lady nodded patiently.

'Good, thank you.' Scott laughed nervously, 'I never thought I'd hear myself thanking a ghost.' His laughter turned into a wide grin, 'I'd have given my back teeth to have seen the look on Naomi's face when she saw you. I bet it was a picture!'

The Grey Lady gave a little smile, pointing impatiently towards what Scott knew would be the British trenches.

'Aye, nae rush lass, you've waited a century to tell your tale. Noo let's just tak oor time. Now I've accepted you are real and I ken who you are, I have your medals in my flat and have accessed your records to try and learn more about you, so I know you served here in France and you took me to see the Casualty Clearing Station. But I just cannae work oot fit you want from me.' In his excitement of having this one sided conversation and getting closer to learning what the Grey Lady wanted from him, Scott was starting to speak his Doric mother tongue. 'I ken you're an Aberdeen quine and that you are secretly engaged to Hugh who we last saw at the Duthie Park in Aberdeen so I'm guessing we're about to see him at the Front?'

She looked grimmer now as she nodded.

Time moved on and Scott could see dawn impatiently waiting in the air to herald a new day in this hell on earth. He ducked as a lonely flare, fired from a rocket pistol, lit up no man's land, the firer anxious for one last look around before day finally broke and lit up the devastation with natural light. This unnecessary expense went unquestioned, despite the British having few flares against the plentiful supply that the Germans boasted each night with their exuberant use. Scott stood back up, 'And by the bombardment of the barbed wire by our guns and the early start this must be before an attack on the enemy position?'

She gave a more frantic nod as she impatiently took his hand and led him towards the trenches.

Scott followed the Grey Lady to the heavily sandbagged trenches. They had somehow effortlessly moved from the desolation of no man's land to appear unseen and unfelt in the centre of a muddy water filled trench. The early morning mist causing more damp to the troops who were dressed in khaki uniforms and kilts that Scott was surprised to see covered in a khaki apron, fastened on the right side, and with a large pocket in the front. He had always thought that Scottish troops wore the kilt and sporran into battle. This more practical solution made more sense. Over the khaki jacket they wore old fashioned 1908 pattern webbing of tightly woven cotton with brass studs and buckles securing cartridge pouches in place. They looked stuffed with equipment; though Scott knew this would be ammunition, first field dressings, an entrenching tool and maybe water and rations. Looking at their headgear he was shocked to

165

discover that they still proudly wore their Gordon Highlanders khaki Balmoral bonnets rather than lightly armoured helmets like the dead German soldiers he had earlier seen in no man's land. He remembered reading in disbelief that in the early days of the war British troops walked into battle with no body armour and that helmets were not issued until 1916 when the Mark I steel helmet was introduced. Troops had quickly nicknamed it the washbasin due to its iconic shape, but it did save lives. As would body armour when introduced decades later.

Many of the men were shivering, perhaps from the cold or more realistically from the fear of impending battle, though few would want to have admitted this. Many hardened soldiers blamed the fever caused by the greybacks, the lice that seemed to infect them as soon as they started their days of duty in the trenches. They were notorious for causing shivering and severe headaches as well as joint and muscle pain. Most reported the pains from their eyeballs being the worst symptom. No amount of heat from a candle on the seams of their clothing could remove the lice. Though soldiers did find it most satisfying when the candle flame heat caused the lice eggs to burst open and they would hear a satisfying crackle and pop, another enemy, albeit minor, dealt with. But these physical conditions were not conducive to frontline fighting. Even the divisional bathing facilities were not entirely effective at removing all traces of these ever present lice. Nor was the expensive Harrison's Pomade whether rarely issued or more often purchased privately and sent overseas.

Scott remembered wearing his kilt to his friend's winter wedding, being surprised at how warm this clothing was and meeting an old veteran of World War Two who told him that his father, who served in the Great War, used to get frostbite in his knees though, since the issued socks with red top flashes never covered that far up. Some Scottish soldiers used the whale oil issued for rubbing inside and outside of their boots as waterproofing on their exposed skin. Others would sneakily drink the rum that had been issued to put onto their feet to harden the skin and prevent trench foot. The service boots, puttees and canvas spats that replaced the more decorative ones worn by the Highlanders were often sucked off a soldier's feet in the deep muddy conditions. Scott could see rum and whisky making the rounds through the crowded soldiers. He knew this was to be drunk to put fire into their belly and buoy them up for going over the top. He did not envy them. It was a double ration for each man, single only being given traditionally at stand to. But this was no order of alertness at the possibility of an enemy attack. This was a readying for battle. Scott knew the signs in the faces of the troops, he had seen these grim expressions in modern day soldiers back in Iraq. This though would be a massacre. No amount of shelling through the night would have destroyed the enemy positions and without proper equipment and the senseless marching into battle in formation it would be needless bloodshed. Sadly the troops would have the utmost faith in their General's words that the enemy trenches would be caved in along with Fritz. They believed the propaganda that they would be able to march all the way to Berlin. Those that did survive this forthcoming onslaught would never again trust their military commander's propaganda nor expect to be home for this Christmas. The steady bombardment from the artillery did not kill the entire enemy as expected. Scott looked at the Grey Lady who he knew was reading his thoughts and agreeing with him.

These men were fatigued and carried many illnesses and conditions that would sap their strength. He wagered to himself that many had frostbite that had been caused by ill fitted boots, the one size fits all mentality of an earlier army. Soldiers would wear several pairs of socks to pad out their loose boots and in an effort to keep their feet warm. Often this made their footwear too tight, or boots that were too small were made even smaller when worn with thick issue socks. Both triggers for frostbite along with standing in the mud and water filled trenches for hours on end. No amount of stamping up and down would aid circulation or prevent the low temperatures. The ankle puttees worn tightly helped to restrict circulation even further, as did poor nutrition and low mobility. He pitied the poor Tommy when he thought of his own comfortable army boots.

Scott jumped back as several rats scuttled through the trench, running over the toecaps of several soldiers who were blasé to their presence. He stood and watched them make their way round the corner of the trench and as they disappeared his eye was drawn to one of the Gordon Highlanders who looked familiar. It was Hugh. He was taking a good swallow from his tin mug. He then jumped up and down, probably trying to get warm. Scott moved towards him, the Grey Lady the ever presence by his side. He passed nervous youngsters, probably no more than eighteen, unless they had lied about their youthful age at the recruiting stage. Interspersed were older looking men, some of whom may well have been Boer War veterans or hardened Jocks from the battles at Mons, Marne or the first assault of Ypres. Some were making wills, using the official forms, designed to be written hastily before battle, just a few words needed, bequeathing whatever worldly goods these men had managed to save. Scott could see the flimsy fibrous identity discs being removed from the neckline so that owners could kiss whatever lucky charm they had attached to them for luck. He noted several crosses tied by string. Other men, not trusting this way of identifying the dead, knowing that these cold meal tickets as they were nicknamed, rotted quickly in the damp conditions had special coins with their name, rank, regiment and religion stamped or engraved on the back. Some wore these specially made ID discs as bracelets in the hope that if they were injured or died in battle they would be recognised and given a decent Christian burial or helped to medical care. Few trusted that the issued green octagonal ID would stay on them whilst the red round one would be removed for administration purposes. Better to trust in charms from sweethearts and mothers.

Prayers were said aloud and silently as Scott made his way to Hugh. Unbeknown to Scott there was a fellow Corporal also praying fervently. Only he was praying for a West wind so that the gas he released would make its way to the enemy trenches and not blow back to his own troops. It would be some months before the German side and then the British devised a way to rocket propel gas attacks in deadly shells. In later years the more lethal mustard gas or phosgene gas would be invented and used to deadly effect. His job was to release the poisonous chlorine gas from the cylinders prior to the advance in the hope that it would disable much of the enemy. It was the first time that the British had used gas on the enemy. Soldiers were warned to look out for the tell-tale signs of an attack which made their tunic buttons turn green. Their eyes would become irritated and soon they would suffer air hunger, a rapid pulse and cyanosis. His only protection, like that of all the other soldiers, was the shroud helmet, nicknamed because it was a flannel fabric smoke helmet that could be rolled out and used to cover the face and head. It was officially called the Tube-Helmet by the War Office. It would be months before proper box gas masks were issued. His comrades preferred urinating on their scarfs and covering their mouths with this soaked rag instead. This was thought to be better than the earlier War Office advice of soaking a handkerchief in a solution of bicarbonate of soda. Though some units provided buckets of this solution for their men, it was not easily accessible.

Another Corporal nearby was charged with an important duty. This was to light many more of the smoke candles which would blow out smoke clouds of cover for the advancing men in the hope that some of them would gain cover from the targeting fire of the Germans. His mate, a Private, was one of two runners, tasked with sprinting as quickly as possible between Battalion HQ and the trenches with important messages. The overnight bombardment had decimated the defences and barbed wire, but had also obliterated the carefully buried telephone cables. Carrier pigeons were also on stand-by in their small wooden cages, waiting for their owners to place messages in their leg rings. As dusk finally fell to the rising of the dawn these pigeons began their gentle cooing noise and scratched about in their small boxes looking for seed feed. Some Germans had learned to shoot on sight these scarce birds at the frontline to halt delivery of vital information on their way to their homing lofts at HQ where they had been carefully nested in over several weeks. They were fed little seed at the frontline to encourage them to fly straight home for food.

The nearby officers were toasting the Commanding Officers of the 2nd, 6th, 9th and 10th Battalions of the Gordon Highlanders, each of whom had different roles to play in this big offensive, nicknamed The Big Push. Scott overheard the name Colonel H. Wright. One CO, Lieutenant Colonel J.R.E. Stansfield of the 2nd Battalion produced his whistle and took out an extra service revolver. This he handed to a nearby Sergeant with a nod of the head. His grim task, hopefully unnecessary, was to shoot dead, as an example to others, any troops who refused to go over the top. Piper Munro lifted up his beloved bagpipes, little realising the danger he was in. His brave example of stirring music, played at the head of this assault, despite being under a gas attack, helped the men across hell.

Scott and a teary-eyed Grey Lady reached Hugh as he was kissing a photo of a beautiful young woman wearing her nurses walking out uniform. He put it solemnly back into his top right hand pocket, behind his pay book, buttoned up and patted it affectionately. Tears were streaming down the Grey Lady's face as she mouthed *I love you Hugh.*

A whistle blew and Scott looked at Hugh's wristwatch, it was 0630 hours. The booming of the bombardment seemed to suddenly stop, and then change direction of fire. Scott knew that after days of bombarding the barbed wire and defences of the German trenches the artillery would now be aimed at the communication trenches to try and prevent the Germans seeking reinforcements to their second position. There were explosions of earth, wood and wire around the enemy trenches, caused by the British Royal Engineers who had spent weeks tunnelling under no man's land and placing explosives. It was carefully timed to coincide with the attack, just after the gas released at 0550 hours, further boosting the morale of the British troops advancing into a battle they thought they had already won. The Commanding Officer shouted the order 'Fix Bayonets!' There was the clatter of steel upon metal as these lethally long blades were attached securely to rifles. 'Company forward!' echoed down the line. 'And may God have mercy upon us,' the CO whispered to himself so that no-one heard him and lost their courage. Wooden ladders were placed against the high sides of the trenches and a young Lieutenant was the first up, blowing three short rasps of his whistle as he unholstered his Webley revolver and aimed it in the direction he expected his troops to follow him: over one thousand yards to enemy trenches. He was fortunate to have the newer Mark

V, but would not be fortunate enough to survive this Battle of Loos, being shot through the head by enemy gunners, leading from the front, just 100 yards from his goal; his distinctive peak cap and diagonally worn Sam Browne belt leather webbing too much of an irresistible target for the enemy gunners. As other soldiers scrambled up on the ladder or impatiently tried going out over the sandbags to face hell on earth each gripped tightly their short magazine Lee Enfield rifle. This was nicknamed the smelly due to its initials SMLE. This Mark III version only held a magazine of five .303 rounds requiring frequent unloading and loading by the soldier.

The Grey Lady followed Hugh closely, powerless to prevent his going over the top or alert him to her comforting presence. Scott followed, not knowing any words of reassurance to say to her, going with the flow of the troop movements as they bravely advanced to the enemy, each soldier thinking of his own loved ones knowing they were fighting a just cause. They followed their officer into the heart of the battle, shells whizzing overhead, the smoke from the chlorine gas inadvertently making its way back to the British lines instead of the enemy position and overpowering those who had removed their masks because they felt they could not breathe with them on. The last Sergeant tucked away the service revolver into his webbing, satisfied that his lads were trained and disciplined enough to obey orders. He reached for his rifle and made his way to the ladder. As he reached the top a German artillery shell exploded nearby. This four inch piece of shrapnel sliced through his face, his body simultaneously being strafed by the heavy machine gun fire that was already decimating his men. What was left of him slid back into the trench amongst the bodies of several Highlanders who had died going over the top.

Stretcher bearers were already frantically running at a stoop to the screaming, wounded men. They quickly scooped up the shot and bomb-blasted men, not pausing to pick up any shorn off limbs. Several medics received bullet wounds for their efforts and tried to apply their own field dressings in a useless effort to staunch the flow of blood. They joined the thousands of souls who died that day painfully in the mud of a foreign land. The luckier ones died instantly from fatal wounds to their unguarded heads or straight through the heart and other vital organs, dead by the time the weight of their bodies squelched into the soft mud.

Scott looked across to their Commanding Officer. He had received several wounds and was lying in an indignant heap in the mud, heavily caked in earth and blood. Even as he lay mortally wounded he was encouraging his men forward. Sadly he was to die later in the Casualty Clearing Station. He was joined in death by 7 more officers and 73 other ranks. The wounded amounted to 8 officers and 310 other ranks, and 1 officer and 116 men were unaccounted for lost in the mayhem of battle.

One weapon-less army Chaplain darted and weaved between the dead and the wounded. He alternated between offering prayers of comfort and last rites to the dying or dead and helping wounded men back to their trenches. They were often simply known as Padre by their men. Though this brave Padre survived this battle, one hundred and seventy nine of his fellow Chaplains lost their lives during the Great War whilst attending to their flock. Three Chaplains were awarded the Victoria Cross, the highest military honour, during the Great War. Dressed in khaki and with only the white dog collar to distinguish them from the officer pips they also bore it was often unknown if they were killed by direct enemy fire targeting an officer, or were wounded or killed by stray fire, shells and shrapnel.

Many of the 4400 who served in France had only been serving in local Parishes back home in Britain days before their frontline duties. Few received any military training or preparation for the horrors of war. Their role was not clearly defined, but their ability to bury the dead with respect was needed in abundance. Many Padres soon learned to make such services brief. Not because corpses that had lain in battlefields for weeks were rank and their smell offensive to even the strongest stomach, but because they and the mourners were easy targets for enemy snipers. During lulls in battle they offered well attended services, men who knew they were to die soon became deeply religious. A more macabre duty they found themselves performing was having to sit in vigil and try and bring some sort of peace to deserters who were sentenced to be shot at dawn for cowardice. Other prisoners tried by military tribunal and kept awake knowing their deadly fate when the sun rose also drew comfort from their presence. Much importance was placed on their roles and in recognition King George V honoured them with the prefix Royal onto the Army Chaplains Department in 1919. Illiteracy was common amongst The Tommies and many Padres helped them to read the much coveted letters from home and to write to lovers and mothers.

The most famous of army Chaplains was Geoffrey Studdert Kennedy who was nicknamed Woodbine Willie because he offered cigarettes alongside spiritual comfort. He was awarded the Military Cross for disregarding his own safety and entering no man's land and running from shell hole to shell hole to assist wounded soldiers from both sides and take them to the dressing station during the battle of Messines Ridge. On his untimely death, in 1929, aged only 46, veterans sent a wreath with a packet of woodbines placed in the centre, to his heavily attended funeral.

After the war Padre David Railton was instrumental in creating the tomb for an unknown soldier to signify those men who had no known grave on the Western Front. This Westminster Abbey monument gave families a place to come and grieve. Some were from this ongoing battle.

The lucky survivors, Hugh included, made their way as best they could, following the lead of their officers and sergeants. They pushed on through the mud, crater pits and fallen comrades. They had been ordered to ignore the dying requests for help, having to listen to grown men cry out for their mothers or sweethearts. The wounded would have to wait until after the battle unless they were lucky enough to be bundled up by the stretcher bearers. Scott felt the cold shiver of fear seize him, he wanted to scream out loud at the futility of the way these brave soldiers went into battle. Not even able to fire back at the distant enemy until ordered when their rifle range was considered close enough. During it all the Grey Lady was crying and trying to make out her beloved Hugh through her tears of sorrow. She screamed as he was shot first through the leg, bone and flesh shattered behind him, cloth and mud racked through his muscle and severed veins. Blood pumped out and he was forced to his knees. Then more rounds from the long ranged machine guns whizzed past him, one taking off the right side of his lower jaw, teeth, blood and bone spraying onto the man behind who became incoherent as he walked, awaiting his dreadful fate. The Grey Lady rushed to Hugh, unable to make physical contact with him but trying to cradle what was left of his face. She watched helplessly as her brave fiancé reached out and painfully grabbed his rifle, still thinking of his duty, his khaki uniform turning purple from the heavy blood loss. Unable to stand and in extreme pain he advanced to the enemy inch by inch in an agonizing crawl that seemed to take an eternity as a nightmare unfurled around him. He mercifully lost consciousness, still miraculously alive, breathing laboriously through his shattered mouth, with the Grey Lady trying to stroke his head, heaving large sobs of pained tears that soaked her tippet.

11

Good Lord but that was so painful. Her poor Hugh, wounded so terribly and she, once again, felt so helpless. This gift, of being able to step into anyone's world, to help them get to the other side was not a gift, but a curse. It did not work with Hugh because he was already on the other side, waiting for her to cross over. She could not communicate with him in this limbo state, could only replay episodes of his life and watch as a silent bystander. She could revisit as often as she wanted any moments from his life, but could not interact with him, nor change history in any way. Whatever higher being cursed her with this ability had a poor sense of humour. Of all the thousands of souls she had communicated with over the decades and helped to cross over she could not reach out for the one that really mattered to her. She wanted desperately to speak with Hugh, to warn him not to join the army, not to go to France, and not to go over the top. But she was being selfish again. She had no right to change history. She knew deep down that Hugh would still have enlisted into the Gordon Highlanders and would have been desperate to go to France to do his bit. No amount of begging would have stopped him and there was nothing she could have done to save

Hugh from the German bullets. But she could save Scott. She could

help him realise the truth and save his soul. He could not be with

Naomi when the bomb went off. Just like in real life she could not be

with Hugh when he was wounded and eventually taken off the

battlefield, hours after he was wounded. His wounds were thought to

be non-survivable and the doctors had ordered him to be laid aside,

given morphine and left to die peacefully. Their valuable time being

better spent on soldiers who would live and may be able to return to

frontline fighting.

Only he survived and surprised at finding him still alive after all

the priority cases had been evacuated down the line, by ambulance

trains or barges, to the Stationary Hospitals, the surgeons went to

work on what was left of his lower jaw and leg. Pumped full of

morphia he thankfully remembered little of this time, nor much about

his eventual evacuation to the Cambridge Military Hospital where

his jaw was rebuilt in early pioneering work by Captain Gillies of

the Royal Army Medical Corps who fashioned and reshaped many

wounded soldiers faces. Against the wishes of the establishment he

spent valuable time, along with dentist William Kelsey devising incredible ways to use skin, bone and teeth from surviving areas and reshaping them into features that would look somewhat normal walking down Gun Hill, past the recently erected monument dedicated to the RAMC officers and men who died during the South African War of 1899 to 1902, and into Aldershot Town Centre. He knew if these men could hold their heads up high with pride then it was worth all the arguing and persuasion with the Director General of Army Medical Services Lieutenant-General Sir Alfred Keogh. Soon Captain Gillies went from one or two cases on a ward to having one whole ward dedicated to his new plastic surgery patients. As his techniques grew and more patient's lives were transformed the DGAMS granted him a new hospital in Sidcup in June 1917. This 1000 bed Queen's Hospital was opened long after Hugh could not be saved, but did mean that she could spend time with him before the end.

Now she must allow Scott and Naomi some time together before they were separated permanently. Selfishly she wanted to show Scott how well Hugh was getting and how bravely he coped with his *injuries. It was time to show him the CMH in all its glory, a fully-*

functioning elite Military Hospital.

Scott was surprised to suddenly find himself back in his comfortable warm flat far away from the squalor and horror of the trenches and the battlefield. He checked himself for evidence of muck and blood and finding none he looked around him for the Grey Lady. *Had she stayed with her fiancé, was this what she wanted from him? Was she finally at peace, left sobbing by the side of Hugh, badly wounded in battle? Why did she need him when she had so easily made her way back in time to be by his side in the trenches?*

He heard gentle sobbing and thinking it the Grey Lady, his confused mind still disorientated from the ferocity of battle and the unexpected change of scenery, he ignored it. As he became more aware of his surroundings he knew that this was not a woman crying out for her wounded lover, but of a scared woman, his woman. Naomi! He turned abruptly to the spare bedroom door, remembering how things had been when he had left the flat so abruptly. 'Naomi, love. It's me Scott. I'm coming.' He was about to force open the door, but remembering that the Grey Lady had acknowledged that she had not harmed Naomi, he tried the handle and was not at all surprised to find the door gently opened to his touch. He went inside and found Naomi sitting on the floor by the wardrobe, her back pressed hard against it, cowering and rocking, her hands clasped around her knees. She was gently weeping. Scott squatted down and soothingly stroked her sleek black fringe and then tried to gently dry her tears with his fingers. 'It's alright sweetie, it's me.'

She looked around wildly, expecting fresh horror to come at her. She focused on Scott's face, now so close to her that he could smell the salty sweetness of her tears. He put his arms around her and helped her to her feet.

'Has she gone, tell me she's gone? Please don't let me see her again.'

Scott knew she was rambling about the Grey Lady. Recalling his first encounter with her he knew she would be shocked. 'Shh, it's alright sweetie, she's gone now, it's just me.' He kept hold of her, gripping her slightly to convey a reassuring sense of protection. With his right hand he patted her back softly, and then tickled the back of her neck. 'Come on; let's go through to the kitchen. I could do with a drink, and I don't mean coffee this time.' He gently took her hand and led her to the kitchen. She was hesitant but followed, only

187

stopping briefly to peek around the hallway, as if expecting the Grey Lady to reappear. 'It's okay, love, she's not here. I'm sorry about all this. I still don't know why she has appeared to us but I think she may have gone now. She's with her fiancé.' As he sat down at the kitchen table he neglected to tell her that Hugh was laying on a battlefield in France, probably dying; he did not want her to be any more alarmed than she already was. 'Tell me what happened. I heard a lot of swearing and banging about.'

'Sh, she was here Scott,' stumbled Naomi, her tongue not getting the fast words forming in her head out in time causing her to stutter. She took a deep breath and sighed out loud. She looked Scott square in the eyes. He could see her old no-nonsense self returning, the fighter he loved and cherished, the feisty Naomi. 'The bitch was here. She wouldn't speak to me. She just kept smiling. I felt that she wanted to take you away from me Scott, so I tried giving her a good kicking, Then she transformed into bones, separated them to avoid my punches and kicks, I swear a moving skeleton was snarling back at me. Then she changed back into a sweet looking nurse in old fashioned uniform. God I'm sorry Scott, so sorry, I do believe you. She really is real. Fuck me; but what the fuck!'

Scott couldn't help but laugh at her, their shared supernatural experiences strengthening the already solid bond they had. He forgave and ignored her swearing, this was a time for listening. 'I'll say it again; I wish I could have been a fly on the wall when you two met!'

Naomi looked momentarily confused. 'She really is real, isn't she Scott. Not a stupid ghost story told by bored nurses on night shift, but a real phantom that can interact with the living world. But the strange thing is I wasn't scared to begin with. She had such a calming presence and looked so lovely and motherly. I wanted to take her hand and follow her. I got the impression that this is what she does and that it was safe to be led by her. But then I got angry and was overwhelmed with my love for you and felt strongly that she wanted to separate us.'

Scott tightened his grip on her hand and leant across the table and gave her a reassuring kiss on the lips. He closed his eyes as he always did when kissing her. 'Nothing can separate us, not even a Taliban booby-trap bomb love. We'll always be together,' he said as he rubbed noses affectionately with her. As he pulled back and opened his eyes he stared straight into the calm blue eyes of the Grey

Lady and jumped back in his chair, the back of his head clunking on the side of the cupboard. 'What....' he exclaimed. That's not possible; you were Naomi a minute ago. How on earth can you be here? That was definitely Naomi I was kissing, I can smell her perfume,' though now when he breathed in he could once more smell lavender. 'Where is she? How did you do that?'

The Grey Lady continued to look calmly at Scott as he rubbed the back of his head, a natural reaction to try and rid himself of pain.

'I'm getting fed up with this silent treatment lass, is my Naomi safe?'

The Grey Lady nodded and smiled back at Scott.

'Then where is she?' He was met with silence. 'I've a feeling you are about to take me on one of your travels again. At least it cannae be as bad as the Battle of Loos. Christ but that was horrific. I'm sorry for what happened to Hugh, did he survive? Is that why you killed yourself at the Cambridge Military Hospital? Did you learn about his death and want to be with him? But you were in France at the time in another Casualty Clearing Station. So what is your connection with Aldershot?' Scott's rapid firing of questions remained unanswered as his head became fuzzy once more and he resigned himself to the now familiar smell of lavender. He was drawn deeper into a dreamlike state and felt himself go into another world, this reality and Naomi all forgotten and long gone as all around him changed.

Consciousness slowly came back to Scott and as his head cleared he looked around him and was not surprised to see new surroundings. Nothing was familiar as his vision cleared; bright lights came in through tall windows that seemed to stretch as far as the tall ceilings, affording as much natural light as possible for an era when artificial lighting was expensive. He stopped counting the windows at ten, knowing they went on further, using this technique to control his breathing and to stop panic forming. He instinctively knew he had travelled back in time once more with the Grey Lady. Unlike in the previous vision he felt immediately safe here, no threats detected, certainly no bombardments nor gunfire. There were rows and rows of metal hospital beds. They were meticulously made with hospital corners, even for the heavy blankets that partially hid the old fashioned metal frames. Scott couldn't help but grin as he thought how proud his RSM, who had given up trying to teach this clumsy nurse military uniformity on the drill square, would have been to see such a sight. Even the bedside lockers were distanced at equal pacing between each bed space as if a long ruler had been used to space and position them. Exactly square in the middle of this old fashioned ward were two tables and several wooden chairs. The wooden floor gleamed, recently polished with what smelt like beeswax. He had heard stories about the thick heavy wooden polishers with a soft cloth underneath that were used in old fashioned barrack rooms to polish floors. They were so heavy to use as recruits sweated as they heaved and strained to move them over the floor in an effort to bring a shine up. They were nicknamed bumpers because of the bumping noises they made. Many admitted to putting great effort into creating a gleaming surface in the hope that their inspecting Corporals would enter in their tackety drill boots and go skidding across the slippery surface to fall on their arses by the Privates standing on parade by their beds. Scott wondered if the nurses he could see busily going from bed to bed were responsible for the cleanliness.

Knowing his thoughts, and equally smiling at the thought of a shouting Regimental Sergeant Major or Platoon Corporal going arse over tip, the Grey Lady nodding eagerly to Scott.

'It's the Cambridge Military Hospital, isn't it? Blimey, I have seen photos, but never expected it to be so big and this is just one of the Nightingale style wards. There must be about thirty beds here.'

Once more there was the nod, but this time it was accompanied with a gleam of pride in her bright eyes.

Scott looked around and could now see a range of patients; those who were able to get out of bed were dressed in their hospital blues uniforms, a flannel type material of Oxford blue hue with a single breasted suit and trousers. As they moved around the ward Scott could see glimpses of the white lining. Some, going out to the end balcony, probably for a cigarette, wore their regimental caps. This respectable appearance was finished off with a red tie worn knotted tightly to the white shirts' collar. The arms and trouser legs of the missing limbs were carefully folded up and pinned back. The white lining showing and giving a jovial appearance in sharp contrast to the white bandages supporting jaw injuries that looked ghoulishly like that used to support a corpses loosened jaw whilst rigor mortis took effect. Those lucky enough to still have feet, wore either both boots, highly polished or just a sad lonely one. Civilians and military alike knew this uniform as the Convalescent Blues and were worn and treated by others with well earned respect. The reality was that the sizes were issued as a one size fits all and that even men with both legs intact had to pin or roll up their trouser legs resulting in the white hems. Most, in time, became ill fitting, since on washing, the flannel would shrink whilst the lining did not, giving a comical appearance that was lampooned by many a popular penny picture postcard artist.

Scott knew that officers fared much better with silk pyjamas donated by a grateful public through various charities. The army issued them with a clothing allowance and a white armband which was decorated with the red King's Crown. Though Scott could see no officers, the other ranks were clearly still separated into class on this ward. These hospital blues helped to remind the men that they were still serving in the army and that strict military discipline would be adhered to alongside stringent cleanliness: the nursing staff could ensure clothing was clean and presentable if issued through the ward. Scott noticed the lack of pockets, probably omitted to save on fabric for these mass produced garments that began life during the Boer War and were still in use up to the 1950s.

Those who were in bed, many limbless, were dressed in immaculately pressed pyjamas. As he looked closer at them he could see a range of disfigurements, mostly facial, as well as amputated arms and legs. Some had healed stumps whilst others were still bandaged, one poor soldier's thick wadding of bandages was saturated in dried blood, a nurse, dressed much like the Grey Lady, though with white cotton protective apron covering her grey dress, was pushing a trolley with two shelves. The staff nurse had none of the scarlet stripes on her sleeve. Scott recognised it as a dressing trolley and knew the poor patient would be in great pain in a moment as his stump dressings were carefully removed and his seeping wounds, cleansed, assessed and dressed; probably carefully timed so that a surgeon could inspect the suppurating mass to see if further amputation of necrotic tissue was needed.

The Grey Lady was smiling grimly once more and Scott noticed dark clouds forming through the windows. Almost as if nature knew there was an anomaly taking place or was judging her darkening mood.

Scott looked more closely at the soldier and though his jaw was bandaged and he had lost weight from not being able to eat properly, he could see that it was Hugh. 'Bloody hell!' he exclaimed. 'He survived!'

The Grey Lady looked down at her feet as if hesitant, unsure of herself for the first time; she then forced herself to look at Hugh. Though her mouth was grimly set, her eyes shone with love and compassion for her fiancé, but her pain was so evident. She walked over to him, Scott following obediently, now keeping silent as he watched the nurse attend to Hugh. As he neared he could see Hugh clenching his fists, mouth tight against the pain that was causing his teeth to grate, trying desperately to fight screaming out in agony. The staff nurse soothing him with soft voiced platitudes as she tried to take off the gauze material from his blood crusted leg stump. Scott could no longer smell beeswax, but the overpowering smell of putrefying flesh, rank, not bitter sweet as some describe it, but foul and nauseating, cloying into his nostrils and penetrating to the pit of his stomach. Poor Hugh had gangrene and this wound care technique, considered developed for its time, was not helping. He wanted to suggest different dressings and techniques of wound care management but knew he could not interact with those he saw in these visions. Scott knew that Hugh would lose more tissue and bone to gangrene in an effort to halt its progress and save viable tissue. His below-knee amputation may soon be higher up, at the risk of losing his kneecap and the important mobility, with a prosthetic, and balance that surgeons had fought to keep. He looked across to the Grey Lady. She was shaking her head and pointed to Hugh and the staff nurse, beckoning Scott to watch and listen.

'You're being really brave and patient Private Wilson. It will soon be over,' said the staff nurse, trying to reassure Hugh, despite his evident pain. A nursing sister approached the bed, her silver medal glimpsed beneath her white apron in contrast to the bronze one worn by the staff nurse. 'Hello Sister,' said the nurse, taking a deep breath away from Hugh's stump, in an effort to rid herself of the overpowering smell. 'I've still to clean through Private Wilson's wound, but you were right, he needs to see the surgeon straight away.'

'Thank you nurse, I shall contact him immediately, please continue,' she replied as she walked ramrod straight back to the small office at the entrance to the ward. Through the glass windows from where the sister could oversee her ward, patients, nurses and orderlies, Scott could see her remove her white apron and then make her way out of the ward, through two thick double wooden doors with circular glass atop. She turned left, the door swinging shut after her.

The staff nurse turned to Hugh and lowered her voice, 'Shall I get her?' she asked conspiratorially. 'She would like to be informed. She loves you very much you know and worries about you all the time. It's not right, you both having to keep your engagement a secret. Love isn't something to be ashamed of. This stupid war robs us of so much.'

Hugh nodded slowly, not wanting to cause any further jaw pain, aware that the delicate work performed on transforming his face was still fragile. Though he knew he must look a sight he wanted so desperately to hold and cuddle his sweetheart and draw comfort from her. But he knew that if he did this so publicly here on this huge ward that he would be causing all sorts of trouble. The Wardmaster was already beginning to suspect something was amiss from her frequent visits. She was a sister from another busy ward taking time to visit a patient from another ward each day. She had cleverly explained it away by saying she was visiting a fellow Aberdonian and sharing memories of their far away Aberdeenshire and City.

'Leave it with me, I'm due a break and shall find her.'

Hugh patted her hand gently in thankful acknowledgement.

''Thank you lassie', he croaked through his newly formed jawline, the words sounding strange through his still healing tongue that had lost a third through the shrapnel that burned and severed during its painful trajectory that took out most of his teeth and part of his jawbone. This kind nurse, and many more like her, had kept him alive by carefully spoon feeding him small amounts of liquid food like a bairn. He knew one day he would be re-united with his love and kept his spirits up and fought back to health. He knew he may not farm again, but he could and would love. He thought longingly of his sheep farm just outside Cruden Bay with its hills and coastal views as he gritted through the pain of the saline wash to what everyone called his stump, but he still thought of as his leg. He looked ashen and his brow was beaded with sweat. His rapidly developing fever caused him to fall back into a merciful troubled sleep.

'Sister, Sister,' shouted the staff nurse, unaware that Scott and the ghost of her colleague that she was trying to attract was right beside her. 'Please stop, I need to speak to you.'

Scott looked from the nursing sister figure that was pushing an old fashioned wheelchair and looking behind her, and then to the Grey Lady. It was incredible to see both, one ghostly in appearance and the other so alive, three dimensional and colourful, but with the same mousy hair and penetrating blue eyes. *Such kind eyes thought Scott, why was I ever scared of her he thought.* She was incredibly beautiful, her grey dress tailored cut to accentuate her slim figure. She held herself with such grace, even pushing a cumbersome wheelchair with a soldier in his hospital blues, both trouser legs pinned up to above where his knees should have been to display white linings to match the colour of bandaged stumps, just below his hips. He was looking upwards and Scott followed his gaze to see the familiar clock tower. Only the sandstone shone much brighter in this midday sun, peeking out around the clouds, having only been constructed thirty seven years ago, not as weathered as in Scott's day. Which led him to think back to Naomi, he wondered what she was making of all this. One moment they were nose to nose, the next he disappears, or he hoped that's what happened. He wondered if she was safe and not still distraught. He looked across to the Grey Lady; she did not look back to him nor give him a reassuring nod of the head this time. Something inside of Scott turned over and he felt a momentarily tightening of his stomach muscles.

The patient in the wheelchair looked down the hill and Scott could see rows of old fashioned wooden huts, probably barrack accommodation for the Royal Army Medical Corps orderlies. The sisters and staff nurses mess and quarters were probably situated in the magnificent houses he could just glimpse at either end of this tree lined avenue. The Cambridge Military Hospital was built on this hill because it was thought that winds would sweep away any infections. It commanded views across Aldershot, not as densely populated as his and Naomi's time, still undergoing construction and development, mostly a Garrison town. He thought he could just make out the newly opened Hippodrome Theatre on the corner of Station Road and Birchett Road, recognised by its still gleaming domed roof, barely three years old. The stalls had provided fleeting entertainment from their troubles for many a hospital patient enjoying the variety shows. He could also see rows of tents, temporary accommodation for the garrison. Even these supporting guy ropes were uniformly in line, hence why so many early barracks were called Lines. He had always wondered why a hospital in Aldershot was named after a County further North and learned during his time in Headley Court that it was named after His Royal Highness, The Duke of Cambridge who was the Commander-in-Chief of the Army at the time. Scott looked once more at the impressive clock and scanned down and up the length of the hospital. It would take some time to walk around on guard duty he thought.

Scott's thoughts were interrupted by the staff nurse, 'It's your Hugh, Sister, he has taken a turn for the worst. He's got a high fever and his leg wound looks terribly infected, like gangrene.'

As Scott thought how sad it was that antibiotics would not be developed until the next world war he noticed the look of alarm come over the nursing sister. 'I'll be straight there; I'll just see Corporal Brockington back to his ward.' She lowered her voice so that only the staff nurse heard her, 'please, give Hugh my love and tell him to hang on for me.'

'I will do Sister, but come quickly, he really doesn't look right and the surgeon may want to operate again,' she urgently whispered back.

'Thank you Alice,' murmured the nursing sister, 'I'm most grateful.'

Scott and the Grey Lady followed her living self back to the inside of the hospital. As they followed a respectable two steps behind and made their way up the ramp Scott was amazed at the size of the corridor. It seemed to stretch for what must be a mile, no wonder all the doctors, nurses and orderlies who were going about their duties looked so thin. This was nothing to do with short war-time rations, but from the daily exercise of walking the length of the corridor and going from ward to department. As they walked back to Corporal Brockington's ward Scott could see brief glimpses of various wards, most looking exactly like the one he had been on earlier. They were designed to house separate Regiments so that cross infection could be prevented and pals could recuperate together. However common sense prevailed and the Director General of the Army Medical Services ordered that they be split into medical and surgical speciality. This included the newly formed plastic surgery ward commanded by Sir William Arbuthnot and where Captain Gillies and William Kelsey Fry performed life changing operations. The nursing sister walked much faster than her serene walk out with the patient earlier and soon had him safely and comfortably back to his bed, two burly orderlies helping to lift him. She made her way quickly down the corridor to Hugh's ward.

'Oh Hugh darling,' she softly cried, aware of the other patients watching her. She knew that most knew her secret, choosing to keep silent about this forbidden relationship. 'Oh please don't give up, please fight this infection. You must get better Hugh. I promise that I will leave the Service and forget all about nursing. Together we can run your farm. I'm a quick learner and I'm sure between the two of us we can make a good go of things.'

A faint smile spread on Hugh's lips, 'Ah ma bonnie quine, I love you.' He struggled to open his eyes, feeling terribly tired. 'Ma beautiful lassie, it's so good to see you. I feel really unwell. Like the worst flu you can have, and I'm so tired.'

She reached out to feel his forehead, quickly bent down and whispered, 'I love you so much.' She drew up a nearby chair, sitting on beds strictly forbidden because it was thought to spread the risk of infection and military etiquette definitely forbade it, and held his hand. 'Please fight for me Hugh; I couldn't bear it if something happened to you.'

Hugh rasped out weakly, 'Aye lass, I shall, but watch out for that evil Wardmaster, I think he suspects we're more than friends fae the same city. I can just see us on ma fairm, it's always been ma dream tae have you bid with me and fairm thegither.'

She looked across to the Sergeant dressed in khaki whose role was to maintain military discipline amongst the soldier patients and the RAMC orderlies. She'd always had her suspicions about this man, overhearing tales from patients that he stole from them. She didn't trust the way he always looked at her. Their eyes met and he marched across to them.

'Hello Sister, I see you are visiting Private Wilson again. Don't you have your own patients to attend to on your own ward?' he said respectfully but sneeringly at the same time, a manner learned from years of having to bow down to officers and gentlemen who he wrongly considered upstarts.

'Good day to you Sergeant Browning, I'm sure you have better things to do with your time than to bother me whilst I read out a letter Private Wilson has just received from his mother.' From her pocket she quickly withdrew a letter she herself had received this morning from Hugh's mother, asking her to tell her honestly and as a nurse how her beloved son was doing.

'But of course, of course Sister,' replied the Wardmaster not believing a word of it and looking her up and down in his sly furtive way. 'I shall be about my duties as you should be about yours.' With that underhand comment he walked off, but not before another surreptitious look at her bosom area, hidden by her tippet.

She shivered momentarily and turned back to Hugh, 'Sorry darling, he's a ghastly man, and could cause trouble for us if his suspicions are aroused. I wish I could stay longer but Matron is doing her rounds and if she sees me here questions will be asked.'

Hugh had fallen asleep, the fever causing him to drift off restlessly. She bent down, straightened his sheet and blanket whilst with her left hand she caressed his discretely and whispered 'I love you,' one more time. Quickly straightening up she then walked off, head cast down to hide her tears, the patients and staff busied themselves to help her embarrassment, wishing they could help in some way. Scott looked to the Grey Lady and seeing how upset she was he did the most natural thing in the world and held her hand, patting it softly with his other. He was momentarily taken aback that he was now the one able to initiate and make contact and hold her for longer. Though her hand felt cold to the touch, he imagined that it drew warmth from him along with comfort. He silently prayed that Naomi was okay.

12

Things had changed and now it was time for painful goodbyes…

Scott ran behind the two Grey Ladies to keep up with their frantic pace as spirit and living rushed to Hugh's ward, their white veils fluttering with their momentum like two white doves flapping their wings in unison. Other QAs tutted to the visible rushing nursing sister in sharp disapproval as she ran inelegantly down the long corridor to Ward 2, thrusting open the doors in haste as she made her way to Hugh's bedside. Screens had been wheeled to surround his bed area, blocking off her vision. She pushed aside Sergeant Browning, only interested in reaching behind those screens, to know all was well. As she pulled the curtained screens aside Scott heard a small gasp from the staff nurse. He also heard an unearthly wail come from the voice and heart of the nursing sister, his Grey Lady. The staff nurse had been pulling a corner of the sheet that was wrapped tightly around a grey and blue looking Hugh's face. Scott recognised that she was preparing his body for transfer to the Chapel of Rest, performing the last act of the respectful ritual of the last offices: they were too late. Hugh had succumbed to gangrene. The bacteria had eaten away into his tissue, muscle and bone. Infection had set in and with no antibiotics yet invented it had spread to his organs, starving heart, lungs, liver and kidneys of vital oxygen. Poor Hugh had died of sudden onset of shock, so easily treated with modern day drugs and techniques, but a killer in the World War One era. Even if the surgeon had quickly operated and debrided the dead tissue it still would have been too late. The unearthly wailing continued. She had now thrown herself at Hugh, not caring that patients, staff or even Matron knew of her secret love. Without him she was lost.

Scott looked across to the Grey Lady. She was staring at her prostrate self sprawled over the body of her fiancé, tears soaking her tippet once again. How often had she relived this scene over her lonely decades, unable to change a thing or save her lover he thought? Christ, who would give someone this incredible gift, but yet punish them with the inability to save a loved one? He thought once more about Naomi and how he would have coped if she had died in the blast in Afghanistan.

The Grey Lady ghost turned to Scott, a strange look came over her face. He felt that odd tightening in his groin and lower stomach. It was fear. He dreaded what was about to unplay before his eyes, but knew he would be compelled to watch. Indeed he knew he had no control over events and simply had to watch them unfold before his eyes, guided by this restless spirit. He yearned so much to be back with Naomi, for none of this to have happened. He wanted their cosy life back. His thoughts were interrupted by the Grey Lady pointing to Sergeant Browning who he could see from the gap that her moving aside the wheeled curtain screen had opened. The Wardmaster was making his way over just as the staff nurse was putting her arm around the nursing sister and saying platitudes of 'I'm so sorry Sister, it was so quick, he didn't suffer and was thinking of you right to the end. There was nothing we could do. He told me to tell you that he loved you very much and that he was proud of your nursing career.'

The Wardmaster sneered as he approached the bed. 'Well, well, well Sister, he wasn't just a friend from your home town was he. It looks to me like the rumours were true. He was your intended wasn't he? I bet Matron didn't know you were to be married?' He looked down with disdain at the prone miserable sight of this professional nurse sobbing her heart out over the cold body of her lover. The Grey Lady ghost turned and snarled impotently at this horrible man who was taking delight at her living self's misfortune and grief. How she wished she could reach out and do him harm.

Scott watched the scene develop, wanting to cheer as the nursing sister gathered herself up and struck the sneering Wardmaster straight across the cheek, the sound of the slap breaking the solemn silence on the ward. The living patients and fellow orderlies taking secret delight at this assault, all silently saying good on you Sister, he's been tormenting you long enough and finally has his comeuppance. The Wardmaster fell against the screens, shocked at the blow. He grasped uselessly at the flimsy curtain material as the wheels moved them further from them causing him to fall to the floor. As he gathered his senses he watched as the grief stricken sister ran off. He immediately rose from the floor. No longer in pain from the strike, intent on getting what he was after all these patient months. She would submit to his requests or he would reveal this illicit affair to Matron. He chased after her, catching the swinging door, spying her as she darted down one of the side corridors leading to the pharmacy. Scott was hot on his heels, dragging a reluctant spirit with him. As Scott reached the swing doors he smelled the heady essence of lavender once more, a headache formed in his temple, all around him became fuzzy, 'No, no, no not now, I want to see that you are safe from that ogre, let me help.' His demands were ignored as he felt himself reluctantly leave this vision.

'Well that's no way to treat a lady, I ask you! Going to sleep mid snog.' Scott could hear Naomi but had trouble gathering his wits. His cheeks felt cold against the table top. He wiped drool from his mouth as he raised his head up.

'Naomi, is that you?' he weakly asked, still trying to focus.

'Of course it's me Romeo, you sure do know how to treat a lady. Falling asleep mid kiss isn't very flattering,' said an indignant Naomi.

'I didn't love, she took me away again.'

Naomi looked nervously round the kitchen, 'You mean the Grey Lady again?'

'Aye,' replied a now fully awake Scott who sat up straight and looked fully focused at Naomi. 'She's in real trouble lass.'

'What do you mean' asked a puzzled Naomi. 'How can a ghost be in trouble?'

'I mean her living self; you've only met the ghost. She keeps taking me back to episodes in her life and that of her fiancé Hugh. She's really quite a bonnie lass and a really kind nurse when you get to know her.'

'Oh yes?' replied Naomi as if questioning Scott's motives.

He laughed, 'No, nothing like that. I love only you, but she is in real danger, there's a Wardmaster, a Sergeant in charge of the soldiers on Hugh's ward who is chasing her. Hugh died I'm afraid. He was badly wounded in France, but survived and made it back to the CMH, back to this building. This kitchen, our whole flat might even be on the very spot where his ward was.'

Naomi shivered and looked around apprehensively, almost expecting to see something spectral, not of this world. Nothing changed, pleased, she looked back to Scott. 'That's just creepy, though I do believe you. Why is this happening to us, what does she want?

'I think she simply wants to show me, what she went through, how she died. I felt her death was imminent but then she took me back to you.'

'I'm glad she did,' replied Naomi. 'Look, let's get out of here, get some help. Someone must be able to do something.'

'Aye, but who? pleaded Scott.'

'Well. I've given it some thought and since we are dealing with something supernatural how about Padre Caldwell? He's a sensible chap, he'll listen, maybe even perform some sort of church ritual to free her spirit.'

'Aye,' replied a sceptical Scott, 'he'll listen alright.' He thought back to the story he told him and how he thought the woman to be barking mad. 'Then he'll drive me to the nearest psychiatric hospital when he hears me ask him to perform an exorcist on a Grey Lady ghost.'

'Mmm, maybe you're right, so what do we do?'

Scott looked up, momentarily puzzled then smiled at something behind Naomi. 'I think that problem may have solved itself lass.'

Naomi shuddered with sudden cold. She looked down to her fingers and hands which had turned blue again. She looked behind her and jumped up, backing away from the spectre that frightened her so much only minutes ago, though they felt like hours. 'Get tae fuck,' she shouted using the guttural slang words of her much missed Jocks. She backed towards the safety of Scott.

He put his arms around her as she turned to snuggle into him for warmth and security, 'It's okay love; you can see her can't you?'

'Yes, but ask her to go, she scares me.'

Scott looked into the pale blue eyes of the Grey Lady, seeing only a calm presence. 'There's no need, she means neither of us any harm, I think she just wants to show us something, maybe together now that she is here in front of us both. Look she's dressed in her nursing uniform, flesh not bones.'

Not convinced Naomi kept to the security of her lover, clinging on tight. She felt those eyes boring into her, drawing her in once more. She felt compelled to go to the spirit, away from the safety of Scott. She once more felt that they had to be parted. She let go of her sanctuary, her lover, and turned around and faced the Grey Lady. 'Okay, what is it you want?'

The Grey Lady smiled, slowly raised her arm and held out her hand to Naomi. She in turn looked pleadingly to Scott but felt an irresistible pull to go to this woman. She raised her arm and took a step forward, Scott watched, unable to move. The two women's hands met and clasped: and everything changed.

Scott looked in disbelief as his familiar kitchen vanished. Gone were the cupboards, sink area and table and chairs. Instead he found himself looking down a small corridor. The high walls were painted a dull green colour and beyond several deep brown thick wooden doors to the sides he made out a staircase at the far end. He was not alone. He could see Sergeant Browning rabidly chasing the nursing sister, who he just spied running up the stairs. But they were not the only ones here. He could hear Naomi screaming, she was being pulled by the Grey Lady ghost towards her living self and the fervent Wardmaster. Naomi was struggling and shouting. 'Scott, I'm over here, help me, she's trying to take me somewhere.' Scott ran towards them.

He turned left and took the stairs two at a time. He ignored the ornate metalwork of the banisters and didn't even use the highly polished wooden handrail, his nager and fear propelling him faster up to the top of the stairs. It led to another small corridor, though this one was better lit, with skylights in the roof letting in small amounts of the fading daylight. He heard a teasing, almost playfully sinister 'Sister, come here, you know what I want. I can keep a secret, if you just give me what I want.' It came from the doorway about half way down. Scott walked calmly to it, gathering up his thoughts, not knowing what to expect, but realising he had to be calm for an already over frightened Naomi. He turned into the doorway and faced an old wooden dusty stairwell. He heard two sets of footsteps above him, one running and the other, heavier, treading carefully in pursuit. 'I see you,' the Wardmaster taunted. 'I'm coming for you, and I'm going to have you, one way or another,' he warned.

'Never, you evil man, my Hugh was worth a dozen of you. Leave me alone.'

Scott looked up as he climbed the narrow wooden stairs, dust accumulated over the years clouding up at his feet as the wooden floor was trodden on for the first time since the area was sealed since the last maintenance man had attended to the clock. As he stepped off the final step he could see the Grey Lady and Naomi, now calm, watching the scene unfold. Naomi pointed to the other couple, coolly accepting that she was watching people and events of the past. Scott looked around him, in the brightness of the glassed domed room he could see four large watch dials but in reverse. He was in the height of the clock tower. There was room for the nursing sister to evade the desperate clutches of the Wardmaster because the famous three bells, one large bell and two smaller, had been removed. Their chiming had been disturbing the sleep of the patients. The larger bell had a twin. They were known as the Sebastopol bells. The other of the pair was at Windsor Castle. These bells were captured from the Russians during the Crimea War. They were originally from the Church of the Twelve Apostles in Sebastopol. Each bell weighed 17cwt 1qr 21lb and was cast by Nicholas Samtoun of Moscow. After their capture as a war trophy they were put on display at the Woolwich Royal Arsenal in February 1856. One bell then went to Windsor Castle whilst the other was erected at the Aldershot Headquarters Office between Gun Hill and Middle Hill. A tradition was started where a sentry would ring the bell, like a gong, each hour. When the CMH was built it moved to the clock tower. The tradition of the hourly ring was maintained until 1914. Sleep proving more important than tradition. The quarterly hour chimes of the two smaller bells, which bore the inscription "Cast by Gillet Bland & Co., clock makers to Her Majesty, Croydon 1878 London", were ceased at the same time. But the macabre dancing figures in the clock tower today cared little for history. The woman in the grey dress, scarlet cape and white tippet headdress wanted to evade this khaki clad figure with his heavy drill boots. She moved rapidly around the clock tower seeking refuge or somewhere else to run to. There was nowhere to run and no other exit. In her haste to flee the sexual demands of this ghastly man she had backed herself into a corner.

'I shall have you now Sister,' demanded the burly figure as he unclasped his belt and started to unfasten the buttons on his trousers. 'And if you want your dirty little secret kept that way you will visit me each night, until I tire of you, you stuck up bitch.' The Grey Lady snarled at this man, unseen, powerless to protect her living self from violation.

The nursing sister backed towards the brighter light of the Northern panel that overlooked the flagpole area. She removed her scissors from the pocket of her grey dress. 'You'll never have me you filthy man,' she made to stab at him but he jumped backwards and gave an evil laugh.

'I like my women to have a bit of spirit, that's the way Sister,' he taunted as he advanced once more at her and grabbed for the scissors. He missed as she pulled back.

'Stab the fucker,' shouted out a furious Naomi. Scott looked to her to explain that they could not be heard, nor help in anyway; they just had to let the tale be told. The Grey Lady looked aghast at herself, unable to take her eyes off the battling couple, reliving her fear all over again. But events unfolded so fast that Scott felt unable to interrupt as Sergeant Browning grabbed at the nursing sister in an effort to capture the weapon and his target. She fell back against the fragile glass which shattered and fell, taking her with the sharp shards. Clasping fruitlessly at air she fell three floors down to the ground with a sickening thump. There was no time for a scream of surprise or for help. One second she was there and alive, the next she was on the ground, dead.

The Sergeant looked aghast at the sight below, a pool of spreading thick red liquid oozed out by the crumpled heap of the nursing sister. He gathered his wits and as he kept crying out 'oh God, oh God' he immediately plucked his head out from the window area least anyone should see him.' She killed herself, that's right she killed herself, overcome with grief so she was. If anyone saw me that's what I'll say, she wanted to be with her dead lover, simple as, I tried to stop her so I did,' said the wretched man over and over again as he made his way quickly from his crime and back to his duties on the ward. He had a dead man to take to the mortuary and soldiers to keep in check. Everything must seem as usual. He had to be as normal as possible. He started to tentatively whistle. The sound grew as he gathered himself together and it became his usual tuneless noise. The terrible scene darkened as the last light faded down the remaining three clock faces. Scott looked to Naomi and the Grey Lady but they were gone.

Scott looked around a third time, but they were clearly nowhere to be seen, yet he remained in the past. *Was he doomed to stay here, was that the intention of the Grey Lady all along,* he thought. *Surely a caring nurse wouldn't strand someone in the past? And why would she do such a thing.* He looked out through the shattered window and down to the body of the nursing sister. She was still in the same position. The pool of darkening blood had spread, enveloping her body. By now a small crowd of khaki clad men and several nursing sisters had started to run to her, not knowing that she was beyond help. Some looked up to the clock tower to where Scott was peeking out carefully between the few remaining shards of jagged glass. He knew he was unseen by their reactions, or lack of any to anyone or anything in the tower. So he was still unable to interact with those around him, he thought. But yet he was still here and all alone. He turned around and was pleasantly startled to see that Naomi and the Grey Lady stood there. They were hand in hand and smiling at each other, looking serene, strangely both at peace despite the horrific events they had witnessed. Scott stood mesmerised. How strange Naomi looked in her mud and blood splattered modern combat trousers, jacket and thick boots in sharp contrast to the well ironed immaculate grey dress, scarlet cape and stark white tippet and dainty ankle boots worn by the Grey Lady. Even the Grey Lady's QAIMNS medal sparkled despite the sun having set and no artificial or natural light penetrating the darkening clock tower. She no longer frightened Naomi or Scott, yet he felt a change.

'It's time to say goodbye Scott,' said Naomi in a reluctant and low voice.

'Oh, okay,' replied a surprised Scott, but glad his ordeal would soon be over. 'Goodbye Sister, thank you for sharing your story. I'm sorry about Hugh and how you met your end, but go in peace now, go to Hugh. Please don't look down outside.'

'No darling,' whispered Naomi, so faintly that he struggled to hear as well as understand. 'It's me she came for, you have to say goodbye to me.'

Scott froze, his blood chilled, but he ignored her, not wanting to hear. He looked to the Grey Lady. 'I know your name. I first knew it from your medals and Silver War Badge. It was easy to trace the number at National Archives months ago. You are Sister Morag MacKenzie.'

The Grey Lady turned fondly to him, a sparkle in her eyes, her smile beamed across in the semi-darkness. 'Thank you young man, I have not heard my name for nigh on one hundred years. It feels good to hear it spoken out loud, and by a fellow army nurse. You're a remarkable young man. Thank you for witnessing my story. I just wanted someone to know the truth. Now you know what must happen?'

Scott sighed, overcome suddenly with fatigue now that the adrenaline had been pumped out of his body with all the eventful visions, 'No, please, I beg of you.'

The Grey Lady turned to Naomi, words not needed, they understood each other now. Naomi knew what had to happen. 'Scott darling, I'm gone, you know this.'

'NO!' he shouted, softening at the sight of his beautiful fiancée, 'no. I love you. I can see you and hear you.'

'And I love you too Scott, always have and always will.' She softened her voice once more, 'But you know, deep down, you know.'

Tears were flowing freely from Scott as he held out his hand and reached for Naomi's cold hand. 'But I can feel you, see you. We even made love the other evening.'

Taking her other cold hand in his she clasped them firmly as if to force him to believe what she was saying. She laughed quietly and said, 'No love, you imagined you made love with me. You still did all your actions with its inevitable ending and I wish I was there to feel your warmth and love and enjoy you, but no.' She laughed again, this time louder to share one last joke with her lover, 'and I bet you did all the things you like to do and some of the things you know I don't like you doing. Did you do the nipple thing, ha I bet you did!'

Scott looked to his feet in embarrassment, then raised his head and pointed all around him, 'and all of this?' he asked as he circled his arm.

'Some may say your imagination, others a dream, or perhaps Post Traumatic Stress Disorder. You've built a fantasy to protect yourself from the truth. Where were you up till last month darling?'

'I was at Headley Court, getting better of course,' replied a puzzled Scott.

'No love you weren't, you were discharged a long time ago. But you know this, you're talking to yourself, I'm long gone.'

'No, I won't accept that, I can see and feel you. You are real and soon we're to be married at Garthdee Church in Ramsay Gardens, round the corner from Dad's. He's even planning on a dove release, he got them from one of his mates at the pigeon racing club. He's been homing them in his loft for weeks. '

'No Scott, you returned from Sierra Leone on the RFA Argus. You were sent out as part of 22 Field Hospital from Normandy Barracks.

You helped set up the hospital to treat those with Ebola. You've never worked at Frimley Park. You saved so many lives out in Africa under such difficult conditions. No wonder they awarded you another medal, you and your colleagues made such a difference and under such trying circumstances.'

'Yes,' replied a reluctant Scott, 'I know,' he finally admitted to himself. 'God it was terrible, the deaths, the suffering, especially the children. There was so little we could do, not even hold a hand or cuddle some comfort into the poor bairns without being suited up in protective clothing and two layers of gloves. They were so frightened of us behind our protective visors, like something out of a science fiction film. It was so hot in all those layers of protective clothing. We could only stay with them, in their tented wards for short spells, in case we passed out, no matter how much fluid we drank beforehand. We just sweated it straight out in the African heat. I felt so selfish having to look after my own health before theirs. They died so suddenly and often in such pain as their organs bled out. It was heart-breaking, but I knew I could come home to you sweetie.'

'No darling,' corrected Naomi, 'it's a time for truth now, no more fantasy. Please be honest with yourself and with me.'

Scott wept, his shoulders heaving with his sobs. After a minute or two he gathered himself and looked at his fiancée, so real next to the Grey Lady. 'Come now young man, it's time to say goodbye.'

'Please, don't take her,' he once more begged.

'I have to young man. Her soul must rest and find peace, only you can help her do this by saying goodbye. These buildings,' she patiently said as she swept her arms around, 'my old hospital, it no longer needs a guiding spirit for the dying.'

'She died,' said Scott is such a low voice as if reluctant to finally admit to the reality of his grief. 'She was killed in Afghanistan by the enemy, just like your Hugh, he eventually died of his wounds from German bullets and shrapnel. You must understand. Please don't take her, Go to Hugh, leave Naomi and I.'

'I cannot Scott, my work would be undone and I would be restless once more. I have been tasked to take the 453 with me on my last journey.'

'The 453?' asked Scott.

Naomi pointed behind her where Scott could make out shadows backlit by the brightest light he had ever seen. He shielded his eyes and tried to focus to make out the hundreds of figures who were dressed in an assortment of modern day military uniforms. 'There are 452 of them Scott, look there's Rory, Ewan, Andrew, Gary and Fraser and the others in front of the Sarge. I belong with them.'

'You died, didn't you? I saw the blast and you fall with the others. I tried to reach you, to protect you, to save you. I wanted to give you the platinum ten minutes. I could have saved you. It's what I was trained for, it's what I do.'

'No darling,' replied Naomi as she reached up to stroke Scott's face, to dry his tears. 'No amount of first aid or even surgery could have saved me or the lads. The Taliban loaded the arms cache with all sorts of nails, metal and junk. It ripped right through us. We all died instantly, really quickly. There was just the sudden sensation of searing hot pain and then this. You need to let me go.'

'But I can't, I miss you.'

'I know you do Scott, but it's my time. Say goodbye, remember me and learn to love again you wonderful man. Get help and be the kind caring committed nurse you always have been.' She took both of her hands and placed them firmly round his neck and kissed him. As she drew back she whispered sweetly and with great tenderness, 'I love you Scott.'

'I love you too sweetie, goodbye and thank you for loving me,' he watched her join her fallen comrades and their shadows shrank and ebbed away.

With tears in his eyes he turned to the Grey Lady, 'Is this real, are you real, was Naomi real? Am I really mad, have I imagined all this, and dreamt it?'

'It's as real as you want it to be young man. For years I watched over my QAs,' she pointed to him, 'even saw men become QAs, something undreamt of in my days. She pointed all around her, 'In death I acted as a bridge between life and death for the dying, here in my beloved hospital. I can no longer do this for I have no more patients and no more hospital. But you have now acted as a bridge, for me.'

Scott inhaled deeply, accepting the reality, knowing he could never share his experiences with another living person. 'Thank you Sister MacKenzie and for the chance to say goodbye to my Naomi, please take care of her.'

'I will, she is at peace now. You have a gift you know. Though I suspect you are only just beginning to realise this. My gift, though I often thought it to be a curse, was to be in contact with the dying. I could not interact with the living nor the dead. I could however go anywhere in the past and present and be a witness. I prayed so many times that God would allow me to change history.'

'To stop Hugh dying?' interrupted Scott.

'Yes, above all else, yes. I went back so many times to his battlefield, to Loos, but no matter how many times I returned I could not communicate with him. I could not offer any physical comfort to him, nor go back further and beg him not to enlist.'

'I'm so sorry', said Scott, 'it must have been heart breaking. I can't begin to imagine how you must have felt over the decades. But what's my gift?'

'Yes it truly did break my heart each time. But I persisted and each time I went back I prayed that I had done enough good deeds in death to be granted my one wish.' She shook her head woefully, tears welling up in her sad blue eyes. 'But I must tell you about your gift young man before I go. I suspect you know this, but since your injury and near death experience in Afghanistan, when you were

231

placed on life support, you were given a gift, certainly blessed. You were permitted to live.'

'By God?' asked Scott incredulously.

'Yes, for want of a better title. God or a higher being kept you alive when doctors and nurses thought you would die, despite their best efforts and modern equipment and science. Since then you have gained special insight, what some may call supernatural powers. You recall vivid dreams about people and places?'

'Aye, I do. I often have dreams and even waking thoughts about a drummer boy at the battle of Waterloo I think. He beats out the marching beat of his drum for the advancing soldiers. He is quite young, about eight I think, maybe a bit older. But he is so scared. I know I would be. I can feel his heartbeat, it is so fast. He thinks about his mother and calls out to her as he bravely beats his drum, knowing that he is marching to his doom. He hopes that she will be proud of him doing his duty.'

The Grey Lady frowned, 'Yes, he is a troubled and restless soul in need of much help. Please tell me more about your other dreams and thoughts?'

'Emaciated men, bent stooped in a clearing. They are so thin. Beyond them I see glimpses of jungle, but my eyes are always drawn to how dirty they look and their tattered clothing. What few scraps of clothing they do wear seems not to fit as if they have recently lost lots of weight. They look permanently pained and weary. I feel anger from them; they are being held captive and forced to work in appalling conditions. They have such resentment but also such spirit, they know they are being wronged and they won't give up.

But as awful as those two dreams are the most sinister has me shouting out, sometimes even screaming and punching out in my sleep. It is an airman, not dressed like in your era, but in an all in one modern jet fighter pilot jump g-suit. He is all in green and with a black helmet. When he comes to visit me there is the salty smell of the sea combined with rotten flesh but strangely with the pungent smell of fresh blood. There is lots of metal work piercing his suit which is ripped in parts to expose his impaled skin. I can see bones protruding from his arms and legs which are bent at awkward angles. Yet he can still stand. A pool of dirty sea water forms at his boots. He does not move, just stands at the side or sometimes the foot of my bed. I know I am asleep, but yet I am awake enough to see him, but cannot move. His face and head is totally enclosed in his flying helmet. It is jet black and shiny so that it reflects my horrified face not just like I am looking straight into a mirror, but like seeing right into my soul. I have never seen such terror in my face before and that really unsettles me. I never knew such fear existed and it intensifies with each visit. Soon I know he will appear in the daytime and not just as a dream. Though I cannot see him I know he is judging me. He thinks that I, an experienced nurse, could have done more. He thinks that I could have saved him. He feels that he died needlessly in a training incident and that the military doctors and nurses should have been able to save him. But his mangled body tells me that he couldn't have survived all the broken bones in his spine that fractured on impact when he was jettisoned from his craft and through his canopy which cannot have opened correctly when he lost control of his craft. Many nerves would have been sheared immediately causing irretrievable damage. He disappears when I wake up, but I am left with an anxious feeling. Lately, whenever a fast jet or large helicopter passes overhead I can smell his fetid wounds and briefly see his sea-bloated body, passing judgement once more.

'I see. But there is more, isn't there, tell me one more please Scott.'

'This is the worst. Some are minor. I like the one of Victorian children playing because they sound so happy and carefree. At my lowest ebb, they come to me and cheer me up with their gaiety. One day I saw a kilted officer hanging from a noose, he had been dead for some time, but the rope still swung. I screamed out in the night. I thought perhaps I had taken too many painkillers for my headaches and was hallucinating. But it was so real. I could hear the creaking of the rope fibres against the wooden rafters playing its macabre dancing tune. Silence all around, it fair frightened me. You really do wake up in a cold sweat, like in the books. I had to take a warm shower, even though it was a pleasant summer evening, you know how nice the summer is here in Aldershot. They are nothing like the summers in Aberdeen where we can get four seasons and different types of weather in one day.'

'Ah yes, I do miss Aberdeen, even the weather. But please Scott, tell me the worst,' begged the Grey Lady. 'I need to be gone soon, forever it would seem, and I do so want to help you understand and help you to use your gift.'

'Well, it's nae nice quine, it's nae nice at a. I walk through a forest, that's pleasant enough. I've always loved the sound of wood pigeons cooing away so I stop to listen. The sun dips and grey clouds pass, the temperature drops, but not around me, just to my core. I've never felt cold like it. Worse than the cold I experienced when you first came to me.' Scott laughed, 'And I ken fine well that you're a good lassie. I soon realised that your intentions were good, so there was no need for the skeletal dramatics! I'd still have loved to have seen you and Naomi have your scrap though. Dinnae mind her, she was just too feart to leave this world and me. I know only I could see her, but she gave me such comfort and helped me in my recovery. I truly did believe she was still alive. I don't think this has all been a dream. I think she was a ghost, as you are, and came to comfort me before seeking peace.'

'I'm glad you are beginning to understand young man' replied the Grey Lady. 'Things will be so much easier for you when you come to truly understand and accept your gift. But the worst, we must share the worst, please continue your recollections.'

'Well, I leave the forested area, seeking warmth. I come to a grassed, sandy type track. There are lots of wheel ruts, as if heavy

236

trucks drive up and down each day. There is a long tall fence with barbed wire on top. I can see lots of brick buildings. So I follow the fence and come to some heavy gates. They are locked, but I seem to be able to go beyond them, then the smell hits me. It's so powerful, even in my dreams, and I never have these thoughts during the day. I only have them at night. They are not so much dreams as the most terrifying nightmares you could ever imagine. But I've never had smells before, only sights and sound. It's worse than the smell from the trenches and the injured squaddies in Afghanistan and Iraq. The stench is even worse than their open drainage ditches. Anyway there are flies everywhere, I draw closer and the cloying, fetid, rank smell follows me everywhere. There are bodies all around. They have shaved heads, sunken cheek bones and thin limbs. They are all wearing the same clothing that look like pyjamas. Then I come to a large pit, and I mean it's huge, and deep. It must have taken days to dig out. Even with heavy machinery it would have taken a long time to excavate. But I can see below, though Christ, I wish I couldnae. There are corpses everywhere. They must have been thrown down because they are all entangled and in different undignified huddles. I hope they were dead when they were thrown down because there was no way they could have climbed out. The sides were too steep and there were no ladders or ropes. Someone didn't want them coming out again, nor found. Can you imagine? The bodies are all naked, men, women and children. But they are practically skeletons. Not decomposed, I think they still lived a day or two before. But they must have been starved for months. The children were the worst. I could see their ribs, but they were pot-bellied from starvation. They can't have been there long because they still had eyes. The scavengers hadn't got to them yet. They stared out at me. Not in accusation but in disbelief, that was the overpowering emotion. They could not understand that this could happen to them all just because of their race and religion. It was a Nazi concentration camp for Jews, wasn't it? The horror was unimaginable.' Scott started to cry. 'My gift is to listen, isn't it? To listen, understand and tell others their story to ease their restlessness. I don't think I can do it, not without my Naomi. I'm just not strong enough, not anymore.'

The Grey Lady reached out to Scott, took his hand and drew him nearer. For the first time in almost a century she pulled another living person to her and cuddled him and comforted him. Scott clung tightly back, composed himself and then broke the embrace.

'Thank you. I hardly ever cry. But these have been unusual times.'

'You will be fine young man. You have coped admirably when others would not have done. They would have been driven mad, but not you. The higher being has chosen wisely. I knew this from the first time I sensed your presence. Years ago I never understood why men were allowed in my special nursing corps but now I do, you remarkable man. But there is one other thing you must do for them all. These lost souls that you dream of and think about do need your help. More than anything you must bring peace for their lost souls. Just as I have done, and many others before me, you must guide them to their peace after you have understood. In my case it is Hugh, I shall be with him soon, and thank you for helping me. But you must understand that you are now an empath, someone who can hear, see and interact with the restless dead. Those who do not understand us truly may call us sensitives, clairvoyants and mediums. There have been many of us blessed with this gift, this insight and true empathy, but I think you are the first who can interact with both worlds; the dead and the living. You have a special purpose, a mission if you like. I think because of your military and nursing career you have been chosen to guide restless souls from armed conflicts. And soon you will be visited by more restless souls seeking help. But first you must rest. Then you must please let my story be heard.'

'Aye, I will, if I can get through the death of my fiancée and the traumas of war I can get through anything. I'll start by donating your medals to the museum and share what I learned through National Archives, people will know you didn't take your own life. I shall pay my respects to Hugh's grave and tell him you love him.'

She smiled, 'Thank you young man, please keep the medals though. You deserve them and it is good to know they are in safe hands. It is enough for me that you know, that you have heard my story. I can rest in peace now. I have delivered the 453 and many patients over the decades safely to the afterlife. Though I rather suspect I can finally do for myself what I have done for others after all these decades of helping their souls.' She turned briskly to the light where a handsome smart kilted Highlander awaited her and then was gone. No puff of cloud, no bright light suddenly vanished like in the movies, just gone. Scott turned to the broken pane of glass and carefully looked out. The body was gone. Instead there was a grassed area which led to rows of modern houses. The sun now shone brightly and along the road a car was driving up to the car park. At the wheel were Padre Caldwell and Major Dunn, the second in command of 22 Field Hospital, who was sat alongside his friend. In the restored clock tower Scott fell to his knees and wept.

Dedicated to the 453 men and women who gave their lives during Operation Herrick. And for those who bravely live with the physical and mental effects of war and to their families who learn to cope with loss and change.

Acknowledgements

My thanks to Bert Innes a Research Volunteer at the Gordon Highlanders Museum in Aberdeen for kindly explaining where recruits of the 8th Battalion would have been trained. If the reader is in Aberdeen please do visit this fine museum (www.gordonhighlanders.com) and do allow time to enjoy their banoffee cake and delicious coffee, which goes some way to explaining my broadening tummy since leaving the army!

I guess she should be first but as it took her ages she isn't! My thanks to Karla for giving me the honour of being the first novel she read in one go! Good luck with the other two that has taken you years to get to chapter three!

Thank you to my beautiful daughter Abigail for the stunning artwork. I'm pleased that my investment into your art degree course is paying off. You are so talented and gifted.

I am blessed with two dear friends who proof read the novel and gave me the courage to let others read it. They are "Padre" Catherine and Ray of Cruden Bay Training Services. Thanks for pointing out my errors. God bless you both.

My thanks to the Grey Lady who did not haunt me when I served at the CMH. I would have run a mile had I seen you! I hope your soul will now be at rest now that your tale has been told.

For more information about the history of the QAs please visit www.qaranc.co.uk and to learn more Doric words from Aberdeenshire please visit www.doricphrases.com

Lastly, thank you dear reader for getting this far. I hope you enjoyed the book enough to tell your friends and family about it and to want more because....

Scott will return soon in Grey and Scarlet 2: The Drummer Boy.

Visit the author's website at www.cgbuswell.com

11043538R00132

Printed in Great Britain
by Amazon